Karen Kimb

Karen Kimball hears, sees, and feels things other people don't… and visits people and places in her dreams. When Karen attends the swim camp her mom signs her up for, she makes new friends and discovers a dangerous mystery at Lovell Lake. Will Karen master her unique abilities in time to save her friends?

"Empowering and enlightening."
– *Children of the New Earth Magazine*

"What a wonderful book!"
– *Northeast Book Reviews*

"Fun, exciting, fast-paced… an excellent introduction for any teen or preteen interested in learning more about opening to psychic ability."
– *Alaska Wellness Magazine*

"… combines the mystery of a Nancy Drew with the metaphysical derring-do of a Harry Potter book – all into one. And it succeeds."
– *Alijandra*

*Dedicated to my daughters,
and children everywhere*

Karen Kimball

and the Dream Weaver's Web

Cynthia Sue Larson

Karen Kimball and the Dream Weaver's Web

PRINTING HISTORY:
iUniverse edition / 2003
RealityShifters edition / 2011

ISBN-13: 978-1456551384
ISBN-10: 1456551388

CONTENTS

The Kimballs

Some children are lucky enough to have parents who dote on them night and day without complaining about what they do wrong, worrying about what terrible thing might happen next, or throwing sudden fits of uncontrolled anger. Karen Kimball's parents were free of none of these afflictions.

Mr. Kimball had perfected the art of long distance reprimanding as if he were in training to qualify in some new Olympic sport. "GET OUT OF THAT TREE!" he'd yell out the window of his shiny black Maserati Quattroporte, as he pulled into the driveway after a long day at the office. "STOP SLAMMING THAT DOOR!" he'd shout from his upstairs bedroom.

Mr. Kimball's three children, Decker, Karen, and Tad could all attest to Mr. Kimball's temper, although none of them could tell you exactly when or where it might flare up next. Mr. Kimball was a tall, stocky man whose eyebrows connected right over his round, bulbous nose, which looked rather like a cherry tomato. When he wasn't scolding, he was complaining. Mr. Kimball could rant for hours about any of a number of boring subjects, such as crooked politicians or how utility companies charge too much. Mrs. Kimball would wear a look of nervous concern as Mr. Kimball ranted and the children did their best to find some excuse to be elsewhere.

Decker was the eldest child in the family and looked much older than his twelve years. Because he had broad shoulders, muscular arms and legs, and natural grace and speed, many people commented that he was going to be a great football player one day. Decker was uncomfortable responding to such remarks, which he brushed off by changing the subject. He often made jokes about that which was painful and once quipped, "If Dad were Old Faithful, we'd know when he's going to blow his top."

Mrs. Kimball was nothing like her husband. In much the same way that Mrs. Kimball's hair was teased into a mass of bouncy tight curls, she floated through life with a unique ability to be both superficially cheerful and worried at the same time. If Mrs. Kimball ever saw sparks in the fireplace on a rainy night, she would envision a fire burning down their house as the river flooded and washed away what was left. Even after such a catastrophe, chances are Mrs. Kimball would smile while nervously wringing her hands, saying, "Look how clean the yard is! All the weeds are gone!"

When Karen was born, her parents had barely been able to conceal their disappointment that she was not a boy. They wrapped her in blue blankets, which showed off her sparkling blue eyes to good advantage and dressed her in boy's hand-me-downs that Decker hadn't destroyed. On rare occasions, Mrs. Kimball went shopping to buy Karen a pretty dress, but these excursions were so few and far between that Karen could count them on the fingers of one hand. Karen usually wore her long blonde hair in a ponytail and in the summer, she cut Decker's worn-out jeans into shorts she could wear with his old T-shirts.

Of their three children, Mr. and Mrs. Kimball showed clear favoritism for their sons and mostly ignored Karen. The boys each had an upstairs room to themselves, while Karen's bedroom was downstairs by the garage and doubled as her mother's sewing room. While Decker and Tad were outgoing and had many friends, ten-year-old Karen was introverted and shy. Any time a neighborhood boy or girl would come over to say hello, Karen's brothers would tease her mercilessly if she so much as talked to the new friend. Karen's only companion was her pet, a white rat named Gumdrop, who she kept in a cage in the garage, far away from the Maserati and its cleaning supplies.

The Kimballs lived in a huge, new two-story home in the exclusive Suburban Heights subdivision just outside Lake Lovell. This home along with the Maserati, or "the Maser," as he called it, was Mr. Kimball's pride and joy. He'd long aspired to surroundings like these and had been thrilled when he'd made enough money with his investments to move his family out of the much smaller home by the train tracks they'd rented for years. The trains used to come and go at all hours of the day and night, and their clear whistle blasts could be heard for miles. After a while the Kimballs had gotten used to the trains and almost forgotten they were there, but they appreciated that their new home was much more quiet – except for the times when Mr. Kimball's voice bellowed out with more volume than any passing trains had ever projected. Now that this new showpiece home and car were finally his, Mr. Kimball was a man obsessed with keeping them in perfect condition, even if this meant yelling about sloppiness or undone chores until he turned beet red and the veins throbbed on his forehead.

The other thing Mr. Kimball yelled about was grades. This last year, Karen's older brother had not only gotten straight A's in his normal classes, but had also taken some courses at the local community college. Karen, on the other hand, felt humiliated to show her father her end-of-year report card with it's smattering of C's and B's, and one lonely A for creative arts.

"Is THIS what you call your best effort?" roared Mr. Kimball as his face turned red, and a haze of dark red swirled around his head. Karen's stomach tied itself in knots. She'd wished she could be more like her older brother, good at every subject. For some reason, tests terrified her, and she would often stare at the other kids around her instead of working on the problems.

As Mr. Kimball barked, "I expect much better from you!" Karen felt a flash of anger and imagined her father with his lips super-glued shut, then felt immediately guilty. Suddenly she thought she could hear another man's soothing voice, whispering, "Don't worry. He doesn't know what you are thinking."

"EXPLAIN YOURSELF!" Mr. Kimball suddenly exploded, which startled Karen with the realization that she had been daydreaming in the midst of his tirade. Indeed, the gentle voice's point seemed to be true. When Karen looked up at her father, she sensed he had no idea that she'd just been listening to someone else talking from the inside of her head. The idea that her thoughts were beyond her father's reach so intrigued her that she experimented by looking straight at him with a serious look of attentiveness, while her mind intentionally wandered to think about her pet rat, Gumdrop. Aloud she said, "I don't know what happened".

Not only did Mr. Kimball appear clueless that she was somewhere else, he even lost interest in yelling at her. With mounting confidence, Karen thought as clearly as she could, "This lecture is STUPID! We should be doing something else now." Mr. Kimball wiped the sweat off his brow, and looked out the window. Without saying anything aloud, Karen thought, "It would be so much nicer to have some ice cream." She knew her father had a fondness for butter toffee crunch on a hot summer day, so she visualized a half-gallon carton of it sitting on the kitchen counter. She was amazed to see that he licked his lips and looked even more distracted. The red in his face was subsiding, and the dark red haze around his shoulders and head gave way to shades of blue.

She smiled sweetly, and he suddenly announced, "But enough of this. I'm sure you'll do better next year, won't you sugar plum?"

Karen nodded and watched in astonishment as he walked directly to the kitchen, opened the freezer, and got out the ice cream!

Karen's favorite pastime was dreaming. When dreaming, she was able to move things with a mere thought and could even fly around. More remarkably, she found herself able to enter other peoples' dreams. If she dreamt that someone she knew was in trouble, for example, she could go right into their dream to help them resolve the difficulty.

She'd once dreamt that Mrs. Potts, the elderly woman who lived next door, sounded really frightened and was calling for help at dusk one evening, but nobody came. In the dream, Karen ran to her window to see Mrs. Potts tied to the post on her front porch. Two bandits were brandishing guns as they muzzled Mrs. Potts with her own sweater. With the simple thought, "Go away!" the bad guys vanished. When she realized Mrs. Potts was still tied up, Karen released the ropes and sweater with another thought, causing them to fall loosely to her neighbor's feet.

The next morning, Karen was playing in the yard when Mrs. Potts was watering her flowers. She walked over to Karen and said, "I had the wildest dream last night, child! It was really scary – a couple of masked men tied me up to my own house, and then I saw you looking out the window, and they ran away!" Mrs. Potts shuddered at this recollection.

Karen just smiled back at her, uncertain what to say. By the time she softly murmured, "I know... I dreamt that, too," Mrs. Potts had walked away to water her azaleas.

Karen Kimball's Charmed Life

On one particularly hot Sunday afternoon in July. Mr. Kimball was catching up on some work at the office, and Mrs. Kimball was busying herself with sweeping and mopping the kitchen floor. Left to her own devices, Karen quietly climbed the mulberry tree in the back yard to escape the loud banging from the garage as her brothers worked on building a boxcar racer. She'd been reading one of her favorite books and had read *1,001 Magical Animals from Mythology* until her eyelids grew heavy. Soon her book was drooping lower and lower, as her arm came to rest on a branch and she began to slip into a dream.

Just before she dozed off, a blue jay had landed alongside her, cocking its head to one side while gazing directly at her. Then it flew off again. She didn't know if she were imagining it, but right before she fell asleep, she thought she heard it say, "Charmed life. You lead such a charmed life."

In her dream, Karen watched the bird fly away. Then she suddenly felt her entire body begin to vibrate. The vibrations began at her head and were accompanied by a loud roaring noise, which grew quieter as they moved down through her neck, past her stomach, and to her feet. It took no more than five seconds for the vibrations to travel from her head to her toes, where they reversed direction and began moving back up her body. When they reached her head, Karen again heard the loud roaring sound. The vibrations continued moving up and down her body for several minutes and then stopped.

Karen felt her right hand sink into her magical animals book. She gently caressed the sharp edge of the plastic bookmark before moving her hand slowly through the soft pages and out through the slightly denser hard cover.

With a start, Karen realized that she was feeling *inside* her book! She jerked her right hand free of the book and lowered her left hand down inside the branch supporting her. She felt the roughness of the bark give way to its softer inside core and stopped to stroke the smooth bump where the branch joined the tree trunk just below where she was resting. It felt good against her palm, and she savored the unique sensation of sap flowing past her fingers.

Karen felt like she was both wide-awake and yet also asleep at the same time. Her body was nestled snugly in the branches of the mulberry tree, and even though her eyes were closed, she could see clouds in the sky and hear a warm summer breeze rustling the mulberry's leaves. She felt the beating of her heart, and noticed that the vibrations that had passed through every cell in her body left her with a tingling sensation. Her left hand was still resting inside the tree, rubbing the rounded place where the branch met the trunk.

"How amazing it is to feel the inside of a

book and a tree, and how very peculiar," Karen thought to herself. She gently placed her right hand inside her book and once again felt the varying density and texture of the cover, pages, and bookmark.

Karen looked up at the sky and saw a feather twirling and tumbling on the breeze. With the thought, *Float,* Karen gently began to rise up out of the tree and toward the feather. She was flying high like the blue jay, sailing along easily without any effort on her part. This was wonderful! The feeling of being free to go wherever she wished delighted Karen, and she flew low around the house over by the garage. She saw her brothers were pulling hard in a tug-of-war with a piece of wood to determine who'd get to assemble the running-board on their boxcar. They didn't notice their sister as she floated down and sat inside the car. Just for fun, she squeezed the horn. To her great surprise, it honked loudly. She floated quickly up to the ceiling of the garage and looked down to see her brothers' reactions.

Decker and Tad dropped the piece of wood they'd been pulling on, and Decker fell on top of a can of nails as the horn blasted without anyone seeming to touch it. Both boys stared with their mouths hanging open and eyebrows raised in astonishment.

Karen flew over to rest by some trees so she could watch her brothers from a distance. She held her sides, laughing at the startled look on her brothers' faces as Decker removed the horn from the boxcar to discover how it could have honked by itself.

As Karen leaned on a tree, still laughing, she

was delighted to see butterflies dancing around some wildflowers. *If this is a dream, it's got to be the strangest one I ever had,* she thought to herself. Never before had she felt the inside of a book or a tree, and never before had she felt so awake while flying around. This was a dream unlike any other, and she hoped she'd remember all of it when she awoke.

Karen heard something move nearby and spun quickly around to see a man wearing a dark hooded cape leaning against the tree behind her. She couldn't see his face at all – it was concealed behind the flap of his hood.

"What's so funny?" the man asked in a voice so soft and cool that Karen felt chilled to the bone. When she didn't reply after several seconds, he continued, "What's the matter? Cat got your tongue?"

He smoothed the lapels on his black satin cape idly with one bony hand while tapping a crystal ball held by silver clawed talons at the top of a long staff with his other hand. "That's all right. You don't have to talk. I'm here to offer you a special deal. I heard you wish you were smarter. Well, you can be. I'll show you what your life will be like when you accept. Watch this."

A sudden wind blew past them, and Karen saw herself walking up a flight of stairs at a university. She was carrying a pack on her back and following students into a large lecture hall. She watched herself choose a seat in the middle of the room, halfway up from the front. As she sat down, the professor looked up at her and beamed. Then he walked up to her. "You got another perfect score today, and with your permission, I'd like to use your paper as an example to show the rest of the class what I mean when I say high quality work."

Karen saw herself nod and accept the graded paper with its inscription, "A+ – Possibly the best paper I've ever seen" on it.

The hooded man turned to face Karen and continued. "All this and more could be yours. If you're interested, all you have to do is nod like this." He bobbed his hooded head without any sign of a face. "One nod and you'll finally be able to do as well in school as your brother."

There was a long ominous silence in which Karen was certain she could hear her heart pounding.

"So what's your answer?" he hissed, sounding a lot like a talking snake. The air around this man seemed dark and cold, and made Karen want to shiver.

Something about this man felt very wrong. If she had been in her body, Karen was certain that his voice would have made her skin crawl! As it was, she was feeling slightly ill, as if she'd drunk several canned sodas and then spun around and around a hundred times. It's true that she wished she could be smarter, but this "special deal" had to come at some price. Everything about this man felt wrong – and yet, if she refused his offer, what would he do?

The Very Small Voice

The silky smooth voice hissed again, "So what's your answer?"

"No", said Karen, in the bravest voice she could muster.

"What? WHAT did you say?" demanded the hooded figure in a much harsher tone of voice. He clutched his walking stick so tightly with his bony hand that his knuckles turned white.

"I said no."

With the thought, *Fly away* Karen felt herself rise up and float effortlessly through the air, back to the mulberry tree. She saw her own sleeping body and felt scared from the shock of the sight. Karen looked down to see her body's chest rising and falling with each breath, and her right hand clutching the magical animals book to her chest. Alarmed, she thought, *I must be dying. I am here and my body is there. That man in the hooded cape is trying to kill me. I'm not ready to die!*

With a desperate lunge, Karen swooped down into her body. She again felt the branches of the tree beneath her and the solid weight of the book resting on her chest. Her back ached from sleeping in the hard branches of the mulberry tree, and she also felt a tingling sensation rush into her legs and move up through the rest of her body. She remembered that she had been resting in the tree with her eyes shut, and also flying around the house and garage.

Karen opened her eyes and, except for her pounding heart, everything seemed normal again. She grabbed her book, scrambled down out of the tree, and dashed into the house, shutting the door quietly behind her. So far, it seemed that nothing bad had happened as a result of her refusing the hooded figure's "special deal." Panting, she collapsed onto the overstuffed floral print sofa in the living room and felt her heart beat beginning to return to its normal speed.

Mrs. Kimball breezed into the room and announced, "Good! I'm glad to see you're here, Karen, because I've got something important to tell you." As Mrs. Kimball looked at her daughter, she set her basket of laundry down right next to Decker and Tad's bullfrog, and Karen watched the frog wriggle into the basket.

"What is it?" Karen asked, as she fidgeted absent-mindedly with the plastic bookmark.

"I've signed you up for four weeks of swimming lessons at the Lake Lovell Swim Camp! It'll do you a world of good. You need new friends to play with, and this will be just the ticket. We have to get you ready quickly because your first day is tomorrow." Mrs. Kimball looked up after she folded a piece of laundry and placed it down on the sofa next to Karen.

"But I don't want to go to swim camp! I hate camps, and I can't swim!"

"Precisely. What you need is the opportunity to meet new people and learn new skills," replied Mrs. Kimball crisply, as she folded a kitchen towel and set it on top of the other linens so all the folds lined up.

Karen would have continued to protest, except she could sense the truth behind her mother's words. She felt there would be someone at camp she'd like, who would be a friend a lot like her. She could feel this with such certainty that her fears began to slip away.

"OK, Mom," Karen replied, doing her best to suppress a smile. The unfolded linens in the basket were moving in an odd fashion, jiggling every few seconds. Mrs. Kimball didn't seem to notice this at all. Her eyes remained on Karen as she continued folding the linens one at a time.

"I'm glad you can see things clearly," said Mrs. Kimball, picking up the tablecloth and shaking it out in one smooth graceful motion. Mrs. Kimball let out a shrill shriek and dropped the cloth as she noticed the frog clinging to it for dear life and looking up at her with its huge eyes.

Karen stifled a laugh, and Mrs. Kimball shouted "Decker! Tad! You boys come here THIS INSTANT!"

Karen stood up and said, "Bye, Mom! I'd better start getting ready to go." She hoped to get to her room before her brothers arrived in the living room. From past experience, she knew her brothers would be in big trouble whether or not they'd left their frog out on purpose. Mrs. Kimball treated her linens as carefully as if they had been given to her by the President of the United States, and she considered any attack on them to be a violation of the worst kind – just as bad as burning the flag or defacing dollar bills.

Karen glanced back over her shoulder to see her mother still holding the tablecloth and staring at the frog with a look of shock as her brothers entered the room. Karen noted with interest that Decker was holding parts from the boxcar racer's horn and appeared to be so involved in the process of examining it that he didn't even set it down when Mrs. Kimball summoned him.

"Why are you bringing THAT dirty thing into the house?" Mrs. Kimball demanded, pointing at the horn in Decker's hand with such a look of horror that she might as well have been pointing at a poisonous snake. "The horn honks by itself, so I took it apart to see if something's loose inside," Decker mumbled.

"Well take it right out to the garage, and wash your hands when you come back here!" Mrs. Kimball sputtered at Decker's retreating back.

Karen felt goose bumps on her arms and legs as she considered the possibility that her flight around the house and garage wasn't just a dream. She remembered that she'd seen Decker start to take the horn off of the boxcar right after she'd honked it.

Dinner was a quiet affair that evening, as Decker and Tad guiltily put on their best manners to atone for the frog incident. Mrs. Kimball's scolding had been bad enough, but when Mr. Kimball's musical air horns tootled the announcement of his arrival home, the boys got in trouble all over again for not keeping their boxcar racer out of the Maser's special spot in the garage. The boys underwent a screaming tirade that only ended when Mr. Kimball lost his voice.

"Please pass the mashed potatoes", Tad said,

with his mouth only slightly full and his eyes averted from his father's fierce gaze.

"Here you go, Tadpole," said Decker, passing the bowl without once pretending to almost drop it on Karen's plate. Karen was grateful for these small civilities, since she realized this would be her last night at home before she left for swim camp.

If Karen's brothers or parents had the slightest feeling that they might miss her while she was at swim camp, they certainly didn't let on. Karen wasn't surprised or bothered by that. She was accustomed to most of the attention directed her way being intended to either intimidate her or impress outsiders, so she was glad that her family wasn't making a big fuss about her going away. She imagined they'd probably be much happier to have her out of the house for a month this summer.

After helping her mother with the dishes, Karen removed her apron and excused herself, telling Mrs. Kimball, "I'm going out to clean Gumdrop's cage and give him some fresh food and water."

"Don't take too long at that," Mrs. Kimball whined as the kitchen door swung shut behind her, "You still need to finish packing for camp – right away!"

As Karen left the kitchen and headed for the garage, she ran into Decker, who stood in the doorway with his legs planted firmly against either side of the wall, blocking her path. "Are you teaching Dumb Crop new tricks, like how to drop dead?" he asked in a low drawl.

"His name is Gumdrop!" replied Karen, feinting towards his stomach, and then lunging quick as thought over his leg to get past him to the garage. "He's not dumb, and he's not going to drop dead any time soon. He might even outlive you."

Karen flicked on the garage light and noticed with a shock that Gumdrop's cage door was open, and there was no sign of him anywhere. She searched the garage to no avail. Near tears and terrified that he had wandered outdoors, she called out his name. She wanted to slowly throttle whichever one of her brothers had left the cage open. Running from the garage to the yard and back again, Karen searched high and low, until she heard her mom calling her back into the house.

"Look at yourself!" moaned Mrs. Kimball. "What are you doing? Your hair is all knotted and your clothes are a mess. You need to take a bath and put your clothes in the wash before you get packed, or someone is liable to mistake you for a homeless person!"

"OK, Mom," Karen replied weakly. Not wanting to deal with her mother's inevitable panic attack, she didn't tell her that Gumdrop was missing. She could only hope that somehow her pet would find his way back to his cage on his own. Maybe he was frightened and just hiding in the garage. She sure hoped so!

The hot water of her bath was very soothing, and for a moment, Karen's mind wandered back to her strange dream. *What exactly did that caped man mean about the special deal? Did I make the right choice? I don't trust or like him at all.* She was starting to get a headache from thinking about it.

Karen's thoughts returned to Gumdrop. She remembered how cute he'd been when she first brought him home from the pet store. She recalled the poem she'd written in her journal on the day she named him:

> "I need a name like sunshine, laughter and light,
> like fairies dancing through the night.
> I need a name so bright and dear
> the world knows it's clear....
> This rat's future's truly special,
> and destined to be bright."

She had sung that poem aloud several times, until the name "Gumdrop" came to her. When she said it aloud to him, he'd looked up at her with an expression of wonder and then sneezed. That was when she knew the name would fit him. Gumdrop suited her beautiful fluffy little rat with his sweet disposition and loving ways. He had always come running out of his nesting box to see her when she came into the garage and would even give her kisses and softly squeak when she spoke to him.

As she dried off, a large tear ran down alongside Karen's nose and into the corner of her mouth. She felt like her heart was going to break from the pain of losing Gumdrop now, when she might not have time to find him before going away to camp. He was her only friend, her pride and joy. She couldn't imagine going to bed without saying "Good night, Gumdrop" or waking up and not running out to say "Good morning" to him. She wiped her tears away with the back of her hand and walked slowly to her room, realizing she might never see him again. She might never be able to stroke his soft, clean fur, hold him close to her heart, or feel his whiskers tickling her neck as he sat on her shoulder.

Could it be that Gumdrop had sensed she was going away and didn't want to say good-bye? *If I find Gumdrop, I am going to take him with me,* she promised herself. She couldn't bear to leave him behind. She would play with him every day and bring him all of his favorite treats – watermelon rind, sunflower seeds, carrots, and peanuts! If only she could find him! Karen needed a miracle.

It was 9 p.m. when Karen finally made it to the laundry room. She opened up the washing machine, dumped her clothes inside, and sprinkled in one cup of soap. She'd just shut the door when she heard a very small, distinct voice in her head say, "Open the door so I can see you. I'm right here."

Karen froze. Her arm hovered in mid-air right where it had been when the voice had spoken. She wondered if the voice was real or a figment of her imagination.

Lake Lovell Swim Camp

"Open the door so I can see you – I'm right here," the small voice repeated in such a way that Karen was certain she wasn't imagining it.

Very slowly, she turned on the outdoor light switch and reached for the doorknob. As she swung the door all the way open, Karen furrowed her brows and looked to the left and right, but saw nobody there.

"It's just my imagination, it's got to be," she muttered to herself, as she shut the door. "I must be *wishing* I could hear Gumdrop's voice, so I thought I did for a minute." Just as soon as she pushed the button to start the washing machine, however, she heard the persistent little voice again. "Please open the door. It's dark and scary out here. I'm right outside the door."

If the voice really was her imagination, it shouldn't still be talking to her now that she recognized it as being imaginary. But if something really was there, why hadn't she seen anything when she opened the door? Karen puzzled this over until she realized, "Of course! This house has more than one outside door!" Tiptoeing barefoot through the dark living room, she padded past the sofa and chairs, the mahogany coffee table, and the grandfather clock. When she reached the front entryway, she swung front door open. Sitting in the branches of a bush and looking straight back at her with shining eyes was Gumdrop! He bobbed his head up and down three times as Karen walked over to pick him up. "Thank you!" She heard the words as clearly as if the rodent had squeaked them right out of his mouth. She hugged him to her chest, and promised, "I'm taking you with me tomorrow! We're going to swim camp!"

That night, Karen's dreams were gentle to begin with, but then transformed into an endless chase. She found herself running as fast as she could, pursued by creatures that grabbed at her legs as she tried to fly and found she couldn't. As she ran faster through a dark forest and alongside a lake, she realized from the sound of approaching barking that dogs were chasing her. She didn't know how many or what breeds they were, and was too scared to stop and look back over her shoulder to find out.

Standing near a large boulder alongside the lake, Karen saw a woman wearing white and holding a stone tablet. The woman gazed directly at Karen. Her presence felt very calming, so Karen stopped running and asked, "Are you here to help me?"

Words instantly etched themselves into the stone tablet in response, "What do you think?"

"I think you might know how to help me," said Karen, feeling reassured to have found someone to talk to, if only through writing on a tablet.

The previous inscription on the tablet vanished to be replaced by the words, "Then it is so."

Karen's heart soared with hope, and if only the situation weren't so desperate, she might have hugged her.

Karen's words came out in a rush, "I have to find a way to escape the dogs that are chasing me. I can't seem to run fast enough, and I can't fly. I feel so frightened." She looked hopefully up at the woman in white and saw her tablet show the words, "Do you wish to be afraid?"

Karen turned to watch the dogs bounding along the lakeside trail, and observed how beautifully they ran. Five German shepherds leaped in unison with grace and beauty, their sleek fur gleaming in the moonlight.

Karen turned back to face the lady and exclaimed, "No, of course not!" Until this moment, she hadn't considered that being afraid was a choice. She paused for a moment before asking, "How can I be unafraid?"

As soon as Karen asked this question, she felt certain that she knew what the woman in white's answer would be. "Decide you are no longer going to be afraid," appeared on the stone tablet.

With all her concentration, Karen let out a deep sigh, and when she next breathed in the cool night air, everything felt different. "I'm done being afraid," she said, as the lady in white beamed back at her with a glowing smile.

The barking stopped so suddenly that Karen's ears still rang with the memory of the din, and she turned to see she was alone near the moonlit lake. The large boulder that the woman in white had been standing next to drew Karen's attention as she noticed for the first time a series of three small markings on its broad, flat surface. *How very odd*, Karen thought to herself, as she walked over to it to get a closer view of its markings. Two small, round dots were scratched into the rock's rough surface alongside and to the left of a circle inside another circle. To the right of those markings was a series of zigzags that resembled three steps on a staircase. Karen reached out to touch the markings, and was startled to hear a swooshing sound very close by.

Karen opened her eyes to see her mother, who had swept into her room and opened the curtains wide. "Good morning! What a glorious day!" Mrs. Kimball proclaimed. "I just hope you don't get sunburned at the swim camp." Mrs. Kimball stopped in her tracks as the first rays of sunshine shone down on Gumdrop. He was scratching his side with his hind foot in the comfort of his wire cage.

"Don't worry Mom, I'll use sunscreen." Karen yawned as she stretched happily in the early morning light. "Although I hope they'll let me sit somewhere and not have to swim all the time."

"But of COURSE you'll swim, dear, that's the whole point of swim camp!" twittered Mrs. Kimball. "I'm sure you'll absolutely love it, once you get started, and then just think of all the tricks you'll be able to do. Why, when I was a young girl, I was a star of the pool, doing synchronized swimming performances with the Musical Mermaids. We performed for the whole town of Burbank at the end of summer, and the mayor himself gave us the key to the city in appreciation for 'bringing beauty to Burbank.' That was the proudest moment in my life!"

It was easy for Karen to imagine her mother as a young Musical Mermaid, since a large framed photo of her by the swimming pool was displayed on the wall. Judging by her athletic stance and flirtatious smile, Mrs. Kimball had obviously been much happier and more confident in those days. If it weren't for that picture, Karen would have had no inkling of this chapter in her mother's life.

Karen rubbed the sleep out of her eyes and remembered the excitement she'd felt the previous night when she'd found Gumdrop. She sat up in bed and gushed, "Guess what, Mom? Gumdrop got out of his cage last night, and I didn't know where he was."

Karen paused. She longed to tell someone how she'd found Gumdrop, but knew her mother wouldn't believe that Gumdrop had asked her to open the front door. Karen decided to skip that part of the story and end it abruptly with, "I suddenly realized Gumdrop must be outside, so I opened the front door, and there he was!"

"How nice, dear," Mrs. Kimball intoned absent-mindedly. She looked quite distracted by the sight of Gumdrop running on his exercise wheel in the cage next to Karen's luggage as she added, "But surely you're not thinking of bringing your rat to swim camp?"

"It'll be easier for you if you don't have to clean his cage and feed and play with him while I'm gone."

Mrs. Kimball pondered this for several moments before regaining her brisk sense of purposefulness. "Very well, as long as the swim camp director agrees. We've only got thirty minutes to get dressed and have breakfast before we load the car and go!"

Karen dressed and ate quickly. When she and

her mother drove down the river access road toward the camp, Karen felt her stomach lurch with every bump that the Kimball's Volvo station wagon hit. Mrs. Kimball barely drove the speed limit, but even at that pace, Karen felt their progress was much too fast. In less than half an hour, she'd find herself surrounded by dozens of kids she didn't know. She glanced down to see how Gumdrop was faring. The small rodent gripped the bars on his cage tightly as drips splashed down from his water bottle. Karen smiled at this comical sight and whispered, "Hang on – we're almost there!"

As their car approached the camp, the rutted road suddenly became smooth. The parking lot with its freshly painted diagonal white lines was surrounded with newly mowed lawns, beyond which were several wooden cabins nestled amidst a blend of pine, spruce, and cedar trees, which gave the air a fresh scent. On the other side of the lake, a mountain swept up to touch the clouds. Lovell Lake sparkled in the morning sunlight, and a flock of crows flew overhead, cawing noisily to each other.

"This camp is very beautiful," Mrs. Kimball said as she parked the car and turned to look at Karen. "I hope you feel grateful for all the trouble it took to get you in here! I worried for weeks with your name on that waiting list, never knowing if you'd be accepted or not."

Karen nodded mutely, wishing she could think of some valid reason for going back home. If only she'd left something essential out of her luggage or neglected to do all of her chores! There was no time to think of any diversions, though, because Mrs. Kimball had already jumped out of the car and was removing Karen's suitcase and Gumdrop's cage. "Let's go check in!"

They joined several other families who had arrived at the same time. Karen felt relieved to notice that most of the other kids looked just as nervous as she was feeling. They stood together on the lawn outside a one-story cabin whose single door had been hewn from one mighty log that was centuries old. The door swung open, and a gray-haired woman in bright green and yellow shorts and a T-shirt hopped down the steps to greet them. Her graceful athletic movements belied her age, which must have been at least fifty, judging by her wrinkles and gray hair. While she was only a few inches taller than Karen, she seemed like the tallest person there, and Karen's first impression was that she was full of surprises.

"Hi, campers!" We're so glad to see you, and happy to let you know that your summer swim camp fun is just about to begin! My name is Charisse Chapman, but you can call me ChaCha. I'll be your camp director for the next month." She smiled as she studied the group of nervous boys and girls, and her eyes twinkled as she added, "If you've been told to go jump in the lake, you've come to the right place! I expect you all to find your cabin assignments according to our master list on the wall here." With a dramatic wave of her hand, ChaCha indicated a list tacked onto a message board on the outside wall of the cabin. "Report directly to the lake to meet your swim instructors – wearing your swim suits! Bring your towels and goggles too, if you have them. We'll be getting started on our first day's lessons this morning, so there's not a minute to lose!"

With this announcement, ChaCha clapped her hands and the campers pushed forward to see their cabin assignments. Peering over the top of a shorter girl's head, Karen could see her name next to the word "Turtles."

"Good-bye, Karen!" gushed Mrs. Kimball, as she put on a grand public show of hugging and squeezing her daughter. "ChaCha says it's OK for you to keep Gumdrop here this summer, provided you feed and care for him."

Mrs. Kimball never hugged Karen unless there was an audience, and she was making the most of this opportunity to impress the other campers with what a loving mother she was.

"Bye, Mom," Karen said, her words almost completely muffled inside her mother's smothering embrace.

A sense of loneliness washed over Karen as she watched her mother walk to the car. She picked up her suitcase and Gumdrop's cage and followed the others down the path to their cabin assignments.

"I'm in Flying Fish – how about you?" asked one dark-haired boy to another who looked just like him. "I'm in Water Snakes," the second boy replied. A crowd of kids walked by, and the boy who'd spoken first backed into Gumdrop's cage. "Oops! Sorry about that," he apologized and then did a double take to gaze in astonishment at what he'd just bumped into. "You brought your MOUSE to swim camp?"

"He's a rat. I got permission from the camp director."

"Cool!" both boys replied simultaneously as

they leaned over the cage for a closer look. Gumdrop was washing the fur on his back with his tongue, smoothing it down with his two front paws in much the same way that a cat does. "What's his name?"

"Gumdrop. What's yours?"

"I'm Andy Parker, and this is my brother, Ben. We're not exactly identical, but most people have trouble telling which of us is which," Andy said with a smile. "I don't think we look the same at all!"

Andy leaned closer to Karen and moved the hair behind his left ear to show her a dark mark shaped a bit like an apple. "I've got a birthmark over my left ear, and Ben doesn't. That should make it so easy for people, but they still get us mixed up. I think they put us in different cabins so they won't be so confused," he laughed.

"It's easy to tell you two apart, even without the birth mark," Karen said with warmth and joy shining in her eyes. "I'm sure I could tell you apart even if you were wearing matching clothes, because you talk and move differently."

"Wow! You're the only one besides our dad who ever said that – and you know what? I believe you probably could do it," Andy said as Ben fingered the wire of Gumdrop's cage.

"May I pet him? He doesn't bite, does he?" asked Ben.

"He's never bitten anybody as far as I know, and he loves to be held!"

Karen unlatched the wire door and reached in to pick up her rat. She put Gumdrop on Ben's shoulder. "Yikes! That tickles!" he exclaimed. Karen moved her hand to retrieve Gumdrop, but Ben quickly stepped back beyond her reach.

28

"That's all right," he said. "I think I could get used to this!" He smiled as his nose touched Gumdrop's.

"We'd better get moving – I see ChaCha coming this way," said Andy. Ben handed Gumdrop to Karen, who put him back in his cage.

"I hope we'll see you again soon," said Andy.

Karen blushed slightly as she whispered, "Me too." She looked down to see Gumdrop staring up at her with an expression that seemed to say, "Next time you introduce me to your friends you could let me visit for a little while longer."

"It was nice meeting you," Ben shouted back over his shoulder, as he and his brother ambled off to their cabins. "See you around!"

Karen slung her suitcase over her right shoulder and hoisted Gumdrop's cage in her left hand. She had plenty of time to look around as she walked slowly toward the Turtles cabin. From the outside it looked a lot like ChaCha's office. It was another one-story log cabin with a few steps leading up to a single large wooden door. A wooden sign inscribed with the word "Turtles" hung over the door, which was partly open. Karen went in and set her suitcase down on a bunk bed. She was pleased to note it was next to a table that was just the right size for Gumdrop's cage.

The interior of the cabin looked a lot like the outside, with floors, ceilings, and walls of dark wood. There were white cotton curtains on the windows and five evenly spaced bunk beds with white cotton sheets and gray wool blankets, which smelled like mothballs.

"Oooh, a pet rat!" exclaimed a cheerful red-haired girl. "My name's Wanda Fane, and I'm so glad to meet you and your beautiful rat!"

"I'm glad to know you like rats. Some people don't like them at all," replied Karen. "This is Gumdrop, and my name's Karen."

"Hi, Karen! Hi, Gumdrop! I like all animals, and they like me!" squeaked Wanda as she pirouetted around the room like a ballerina, the skirt on her swimsuit fanning out around her.

A few other girls had already thrown their suitcases down on their bunks and changed. A tall, muscular brunette smiled at Karen. "Hi! Glad to meet you! I'm Miranda!" she said before grabbing her goggles and sauntering out of the cabin. "I'll see you out there!" she yelled over her shoulder. Two more girls walked in as Miranda left.

"Hi, snappy Turtles!" said a black girl with long thin beaded braids, "We Turtles are known for our STYLE! Isn't that right, Gina?" She gave the shorter blonde next to her a high-five, which seemed to catch her off-guard and nearly toppled her. "I'm Julie Keble, and this here is my new friend Gina Dardani!"

"Hi Julie and Gina!" said Karen and Wanda together. They looked at each other and laughed. They hadn't been trying to sing a chorus!

Julie and Gina carried their suitcases to the bunk bed nearest Karen and Wanda and began to settle in. Karen noted with interest that Julie seemed to have at least twice as much luggage as the other campers, and that each piece was made from matching tweed material and emblazoned with the monogrammed initials, "J.A.K." on shiny brass faceplates.

Gina struggled unsuccessfully to open her suitcase latch. "I wish this would open for me," she said softly in a foreign accent. "My suitcase, she is always getting stuck."

"Here, let me help you," Julie offered, springing to Gina's side. "It looks like you need a key to open this. Is it locked?"

"No, I didn't lock it. I just shut it and CLICK!"

"Well, I've seen a lot of luggage, and I can assure you that this one is locked," Julie replied. "Don't you worry, though. I've got the touch." Julie opened one of her smaller bags and retrieved a small box of tools. "I love to be prepared, so I carry something for every occasion!" She inserted a thin instrument into the lock, and deftly jiggled it until a "CLICK!" was heard and the suitcase sprang open.

"Grazie! Thank you very much, Julie!" Gina gushed, her brown eyes shining with gratitude.

"My pleasure!" Julie replied, returning her tool kit to her bag. Karen watched Gina brush her long, dark hair into a ponytail, and asked her, "Where are you from originally?"

"I grew up in Italy, and my family, we move-ed to A-may-ree-kah last year."

"How do you like it so far?"

"Very much!"

Julie whistled a happy tune as she opened her suitcase and dumped the contents on her bed, grabbed her goggles and swimsuit and dashed to the bathroom. "Last one to the lake is a rubber ducky!"

As soon as the bathroom was free, Karen changed quickly into her swimsuit. She was grateful to see that Wanda was still in the cabin.

"Thanks for waiting for me!"

"What are friends for?" laughed Wanda, as the two girls made their way down the steps to the dirt trail leading to their very first swim lesson at Lovell lake.

Swimming Lessons

When they arrived at the lake, most of the other campers were already there. Everyone gathered around ChaCha, who was holding an orange flotation device above her head. She blew three short blasts on the gold-colored whistle she wore on a rope around her neck and shouted, "May I have your attention, please! The Lake Lovell Swim Camp has now officially begun! I am proud to announce your swimming instructors: Steve! Sondra! Mike! And Jasper!"

As ChaCha announced the instructor's names, they walked up to stand alongside her, bowing their heads like performers at the end of a play. They all appeared to be in their early twenties and looked like college students who had taken swim camp instructor jobs to earn some extra money in the summer.

Steve was a blonde-haired muscular young man with movie-star good looks, complete with stylish sunglasses and perfectly trimmed hair. Sondra was petite with glasses and long dark hair that fell over them when she bowed. Mike was covered in soft curly brown hair that didn't stop at his neck, but seemed to cover every inch of his body. Jasper was a blonde with hair shorter than that of most boys. Her ears sparkled with bangles, ear cuffs and studs of every size and shape.

ChaCha blew her whistle again to quiet the campers, who had been chattering as the swim instructors made their grand entrance. "Everyone in Flying Fish, please line up next to Steve. All Turtles line up behind Sondra... all River Otters behind Jasper... and all Water Snakes line up behind Mike!"

Amid loud squeals of excitement and much talking, the campers fell into place behind the instructor for their group. Andy waved at Karen before joining the line behind Steve with the other Flying Fish. Steve combed his hair, flipping his bangs back into just the right position before pocketing his comb in his sleek designer racing swim trunks. Much to Karen's amusement, Andy mimicked each and every one of Steve's grooming motions, including the distant gaze in his eyes and the way he held his chin up high. Andy looked up to see Karen smile at him, and he grinned back.

Karen glanced to her right and was pleased to see that she was still with Wanda, who continued to pirouette around and around in excitement. "Did you see our instructor?" she breathed heavily. "Is she skinny or what! I hope she doesn't lose her glasses in the lake!" Karen had been wondering the same thing. It seemed a bit odd for a swim instructor to wear glasses instead of contacts.

ChaCha blew her whistle for a long third blast until all four groups of swim campers turned to face her. "What a lovely group of campers we have assembled here today!" she beamed. "Please note that you are to stay with your group at all times during swim practice, and under no circumstances are allowed on the far side of the lake, past the buoys."

"Why not? What's over there that we're not supposed to see?" asked a skinny boy with freckles and a sun visor.

"It's a matter of safety," ChaCha replied. All campers must stay close to camp and medical care. Now that you're all in your groups, let's get started swimming!"

Karen, Wanda, and eight other Turtles followed their leader to a sandy part of the beach, where they listened to Sondra explain the basics of water safety.

"Always stay in sight of your partner. Remember that you can hold your breath and float if you are in deep water and need to rest. I'll start today's lessons with kick boards for our beginning swimmers. If you don't know how to swim, come and get a board. More advanced people can warm up by swimming out to the raft and back while the beginners get their feet wet!" Sondra paused to smile at her own joke and continued, "Use your feet and hands any way you like. We'll work on style later!"

Without a moment's hesitation, Miranda and five other girls dove into the lake and swam out toward the raft. "Heather! Kimberly!" Sondra yelled out after blonde and brunette haired girls. "You left your goggles on the beach. Do you want them?"

"No," they both replied.

"They're not safe on the ground, they might get stepped on," Sondra called back, "So I'll keep them with the kick boards."

"Thank you!" the blonde answered.

Julie, Gina, Karen, and Wanda walked barefoot over the warm sand to select their kick boards, and then walked back again. Karen loved the feel of sand between her toes and the way the sunlight sparkled so brightly on the water. She also liked Sondra's easy-going approach to the swimming lesson and tried to imagine her as a Musical Mermaid, doing synchronized swimming alongside Mrs. Kimball. Somehow, Karen just couldn't picture it, and this brought a huge smile to her face.

"Beginning swimmers need buddies!" Sondra called out joyfully. "Please pick your buddy and come on into the water!" Karen felt immediately at ease and was grateful that Sondra was her instructor. Karen and Wanda exchanged glances as they waded into the lake, the soft mud oozing up between their toes. "Watch out for the giant sucker fish!" shouted Julie. "He's got squishy skin that sucks you in – and then he gobbles you whole!" The Turtles were uniformly surprised and disgusted as they discovered how gooey the lake bottom was. They did little to hide their revulsion.

"EEK!" squealed Gina, jumping backwards out of the water. Julie laughed so hard she fell down and was pulled upright again by Karen and Wanda.

"Find your partner, and hold hands up to show who's got a buddy and who still needs one," Sondra called out in her melodious voice.

"You're my buddy!" exclaimed Wanda, reaching for Karen's hand. Karen smiled, and looked around to see that Julie and Gina were partners and that Miranda and the rest of the Turtles who knew how to swim were already heading out to the raft.

"Let's start by practicing our kicks on the

kick boards to get the feel of it. Hold on to your board with both hands, and KICK!" Sondra demonstrated for a few seconds and then stood up. "Now you try it!"

Karen looked at Wanda. "Ready?" Both girls giggled and leaned forward onto their boards. A huge spray of water splashed up behind Wanda, as her legs pounded the surface of the lake. "Keep your feet under water, and you'll splash less and go faster," said Sondra.

"I don't want to go faster – I just don't want to DROWN," wailed Wanda.

Karen saw that Julie was lying down on her kick board, floating along with occasional kicks.

"Put your board out in front of you and hold it with both arms outstretched," Sondra reminded her. Julie pouted and slid off of her board. Sondra spoke in a louder voice to address the entire group of beginning swimming Turtles. "The boards are here to help us gain confidence as we practice our kicks. We are just using them to hold onto while we learn what it feels like to move through the water."

A few minutes later, the experienced swimmers returned to the shore. Karen got an uneasy feeling that Miranda, Heather, and the other girls were laughing at how the beginners were using kick boards. "Do you think they're laughing at us?" Karen asked Wanda.

Wanda looked up from her board at the experienced swimmers, raising her right hand above her eyes as a visor. "I hope not. They might just be laughing because they're having fun."

Sondra called out to the experienced swimmers, "Keep on going! Back to the raft again!" There was a collective moan as Miranda, Heather, Kimberly and the other older girls turned to swim back out toward the middle of the lake.

Karen turned to Wanda and said, "They're not having *that* much fun... I think they were making fun of us."

Sondra announced, "Now we'll swim on our backs with the boards stretched out ahead of us."

"This is fun! I can see the clouds and birds!" squealed Wanda to Karen as she looked up into the blue sky above.

Karen called back, "I know! I love it!" She loved the feeling of warm air and cool water together and loved smelling the fresh clean scent of pine and cedar. So far, swimming was not as frightening as she'd thought it might be.

"OK beginners! Let's practice bouncing in the water, so our whole body goes under water, then our face comes up, and we get a breath," Sondra announced to the beginners. She began bouncing up and down, disappearing under water and gasping for air each time she broke the surface. Wanda, Gina, Julie, and Karen began bouncing and sputtering and soon had the same rhythm as Sondra.

After about twenty bounces, Sondra said, "And now we'll try out a simple swim stroke – the dog paddle! All you have to do is kick like you did on your boards and paddle like a dog." Sondra moved her arms in a circle, much the same way that one's feet move while peddling a bicycle.

"I can't believe how easy this is – I used to be afraid of the water!" exclaimed Karen, as her head bobbed up and down in the waves of the lake with each stroke of her arms.

"I can't talk... and swim... at the same time!" gasped Wanda. "HELP! I'm drowning!" Wanda's head went under water for a moment, and then she sputtered back to the surface, kicking with furious resolve.

Sondra rushed to Wanda's side and said in an authoritative voice, "Wanda, you're doing just fine. Keep paddling and kicking and don't stop, even if you are talking. As long as you keep paddling and kicking, you won't drown."

"Promise?" Wanda gasped.

"I promise!"

"Watch this!" Karen called out to Wanda, "I'm going to swim under water. It's a lot like flying... through syrup!" Wanda giggled and somehow managed to keep kicking as she laughed.

When Karen surfaced, she looked at the far side of the lake and got goose bumps as she noticed that it seemed very familiar. A large boulder with a flat face on the far side of the lake looked exactly like the one in her dream! Even though it was a long distance away, Karen was certain it was the same. She squinted and put a hand over her eyes to see if she could recognize the unusual markings. It was hard to tell for sure, but she thought she could just make out the circle inside the circle!

"What are you staring at?" Wanda asked so abruptly that Karen jumped.

"That rock over there. It seems to have some unusual markings on it."

"Where? I can't see them!" Wanda squinted so fiercely that her nose scrunched up as if she had sniffed something foul in the air.

Karen grinned as she replied, "It's probably nothing. And besides, ChaCha said that the far side of the lake is off limits."

"TWEET!" blew Sondra's whistle, signaling the end of the afternoon swim. "Time to go back in, shower, and change for dinner!"

"Thank goodness, I'm starving!" said Karen to Wanda as the two girls headed back to the Turtle cabin.

Campers lined up in the huge mess hall to get their plates, silverware, and trays in the cafeteria-style serving line and then sat together in the same groups they were assigned to by cabin. The mess hall was the largest cabin at Lake Lovell Swim Camp, although it was made of the same dark wooden beams, flooring, and walls. Huge picture windows on the west wall provided a breathtaking view of the sun setting behind the mountains on the other side of the lake. Pink and orange clouds embraced the shoulders of the mountain like fluffy blankets as the sun sank lower and lower on the horizon. The man and woman dishing out the food were efficient and friendly and served the campers and staff fast enough to keep the dinner line moving at a good speed. Karen was glad to see Andy and Ben in line next to her and grinned as Andy again mimicked Steve's grooming routine.

Ben commented in a low conspiratorial voice to Andy, "At least your swim instructor keeps his eyes on the water. Mike seems more interested in the girls!" to which Andy responded by pantomiming Mike looking longingly off in the distance with one hand tucked under his shirt rising and falling to mimic the pounding of a heart in love.

Karen laughed at the twins' impromptu comedy routine, and said, "I like Sondra. She's a great teacher. This was my first day learning how to swim, and I was scared until she told me to just relax and kick and paddle any way I liked."

"Sondra seems nice," Andy agreed and then fell silent as several boys trudged over to join the line behind them. Karen could tell by Andy's expression that he was less than thrilled with their arrival, and she thought she remembered some of them from his Flying Fish group.

"Aren't those boys part of your team?" she whispered.

Andy nodded, and Karen saw from the somber look on his face that he was no longer in any mood to talk. She murmured, "See you later!" and took her plate of food over to join Wanda and the other Turtles at their table. Dinner was a simple meal of spaghetti, garlic bread, and salad, but it tasted divine to Karen after a hard day of swimming lessons. The girls at the table laughed and chatted about the day's events as they ate, and Karen felt herself beginning to relax. She marveled at how some kids loved to tell jokes and stories. Karen preferred to listen. If she hadn't met Wanda, she knew she'd probably be completely silent at dinner, but Wanda kept making jokes and comments and asking Karen questions like, "Who's your favorite swim instructor?"

Karen's one word responses like, "Sondra," did little to discourage Wanda's cheerful banter. Toward the end of the meal, ChaCha blew two short blasts on her golden whistle and said,

"Now it's time for us to join our voices together in song! Those of you who know the Lovell Lake Swim Camp song can sing along, and the rest of you can learn it – it's short and sweet – just like me!" She cleared her throat as a hush fell across the room, and in a voice as clear as a bell began to sing,

> *"Lovell Lake calls to me*
> *High in the mountains, far from the sea.*
> *New friends and old all come together*
> *To splash and play in summer weather*
> *When days are long and nights are short*
> *And swimming is our favorite sport.*
> *We brave brown mud and slimy goo,*
> *And swim in water clear and blue!"*

As ChaCha ended the song accompanied by some of the older swim campers, she took a deep bow to much laughter and applause. Then she said, "Good night everyone!" and waved at the crowd of campers before sauntering outside into the crisp night air. The fresh smells of pine and cedar wafted into the mess hall, reminding Karen of how much she wanted to walk back to her cabin and see Gumdrop before going to bed.

Karen followed the other Turtles along the path to their cabin and looked forward to climbing into her bunk. After brushing her teeth and changing into her nightgown, she finally had some time to herself. Karen turned her head to look at Gumdrop, and saw him stand up on his hind legs, holding the bars of his cage and looking back at her. She unfastened the wire door and watched Gumdrop take a few tentative steps outside the safety of his cage. She scooped him up and set him down on a towel she'd spread out on her bed so he could walk around and investigate. Karen patted Gumdrop and made a "cave" out of one corner of the towel. She giggled as he played hide-and-go-seek with her, tucking himself into the folds of the towel. Then his nose would protrude from the cave entrance, and his whiskers would quiver as he looked up expectantly into Karen's eyes.

"Do you want a hug?" she asked, as she scooped him up and snuggled him close to her face in both hands. His fur felt soft and warm against her cheek, and his whiskers tickled her face, making her giggle again.

A soft voice behind Karen said, "Your little rat, he is so cute! How old is he?" Karen turned to see Gina watching her, and replied, "He's six months old."

"Shh!" hissed Heather from across the cabin, glaring at Gina and Karen. The older girls were all reading books or writing in journals, and apparently guarded their quiet time fiercely. Gina shuffled off to her bunk, and Karen gave her rat a good night kiss. "I think it's time for bed," Karen whispered, as she sat Gumdrop gently back inside his cage and fastened the door. "Good night, Gumdrop." She looked out the window. There was something very strange about this place, and about her recent dreams. She felt like she was on the verge of understanding a deep mystery – and facing something terrifying. She shut her eyes and prepared to drift off.

Just before the dream began, Karen felt the familiar vibrations and heard the loud roaring sound. She was so tired from swimming that she didn't attempt to move, so she was shocked when suddenly without warning she felt her back bump up against something solid behind her. She reached around to feel what it was, and touched the rough edges of wooden beams bumping her elbows. Her fingers explored further, and she felt smooth flat expanses between the wooden beams. She was floating up at the top of the cabin with her back bumping into the ceiling!

Looking down, Karen saw Gumdrop in his cage, getting a drink of water from his bottle. She noticed that every bed in the Turtle cabin was occupied. There even seemed to be someone in her bed. With a jolt, Karen realized she was looking at her own body! She felt fully awake now and increasingly nervous. She remembered that the last time she'd seen her body in a dream, when she'd met the very unpleasant man. He didn't seem to be anywhere in sight, and she didn't feel like she was dying, so Karen figured this would be a great opportunity to fly around the lake. Cautiously, she poked her arm up through the ceiling of the cabin and felt cool night air on the other side. With the thought, "Rise," she flew up out of the cabin. Floating higher above the roof to get a full view of the lake, she rested for a moment. What a joy it was to be flying again!

She stretched her arms and legs and looked back down through the window. In spite of the fact that it was dark, she could see Gumdrop take a seed from his food bowl and retreat to his Kleenex box. She then gazed out across the lake to the mountains on the other side.

Karen felt the far side of the lake calling to

her, so she flew toward it above the sparkling moonlit waters of Lake Lovell. She looked down at the water's surface to see if her reflection was dancing on the silver waters, but all she saw was the brilliant reflection of the moon. As a cloud glided across the moon, Karen could see she had almost reached the large boulder. She slowed down and hovered for a moment alongside the boulder before gently touching down to Earth. There were those strange markings: the two dots, the circle within the circle, and the three steps. They seemed to have been carved here for a reason, many years ago. Karen turned and stood next to the boulder, looking around to see if there was anything else unusual about this place. The mountain's rocky wall rose straight up from the ground to the darkening clouds overhead, with occasional bushes and small trees to decorate its majestic presence. Most of the bushes and trees were down low on the mountain, but none of them stood out as being anything particularly special. Karen traced the markings with her index finger, beginning with the two dots and ending with the zigzag steps.

Clouds had now gathered in a big cluster in front of the moon as if a storm were on its way. But these clouds didn't look like regular storm clouds. They were darker than any Karen had ever seen. They writhed and roiled as if they were filled with snakes, and rumbled and boomed with occasional flashes of lightning sparking in the darkness of their depths. Somewhere within the rumblings of the cloud, she heard a man's voice growling, "Go away!" The storm was headed straight toward her cabin.

Ohgeenay

Hovering on the far side of the lake in her waking dream, Karen felt herself torn in two as she watched the terrifying storm approach. Half of her wanted to return to her sleeping body in the cabin, while the other half longed to fly away from the monstrous storm. To fly off now would be to abandon herself, which was what the voice of the storm was demanding that she do.

Her mind raced. "Why would someone want me to fly away and leave my body behind?" Karen asked herself. That would be saving her dream self but abandoning her body, not to mention Gumdrop and her new friends. Something else seemed to be trying to take over her body, and she didn't want that to happen. Karen realized that she had to make a choice. She could either fly away and keep her mind and spirit free, or return to her body and face the demonic storm.

A male voice boomed, "Go now, before it is too late!"

Karen shook her head. "No!" She realized that she'd made up her mind. She was going to stay.

The clouds covered the entire sky now, blocking out the moon and stars. A wild wind flung leaves and twigs in all directions, and raised white caps on peaked waves across the lake. Karen braced herself to face the storm, and flew back across the choppy waters toward the dark cloud approaching the cabins. From within the cloud emerged a dark caped figure that looked strangely familiar. He floated down closer and closer, blocking her return to her cabin. "Go now, while you still can," he snarled as one of his bony hands touched Karen's. Karen gasped as his icy touch chilled her to the core. She felt goose bumps rising up on her arms and legs, and yanked her arm away.

"Who ARE you?" Karen demanded, looking into the dark area under the hood in an attempt to see his face. There appeared to be a head holding the hood up, but inside seemed to be just black empty space.

The figure remained silent for several moments as the wind howled around them, and then in a voice so low that Karen could barely hear it, the caped man grumbled, "I am Ohgeenay."

His voice had an odd effect on Karen, and for a moment she was fixed in place, listening closely to his words. The name was like nothing she'd ever heard; it was strange, like Ohgeenay himself.

Lightning flashed across the sky, and for the briefest moment, Karen glimpsed his face. His shriveled skin was rough like an old apple, and his beady eyes were set in red-rimmed sockets. She could not read the expression on his face, nor the meaning of a strange hand gesture he made as his left hand lifted his staff high above his head, and his right hand opened towards her, just behind the crystal ball atop his staff.

"I have been waiting for you for a long time,

Karen Kimball," Ohgeenay rasped. "You have not seen me, but I have watched you grow from a baby into a young girl. There will come a time when you will understand that you need me, and you will summon me of your own free will."

Karen thought to herself, *Fat chance!*

"I have seen it, and so it will be," Ohgeenay declared, as he lowered his staff and another flash of lightning illuminated his wrinkled face.

"Never!" Karen whispered under her breath, and quickly returned to her cabin. With a thought, she floated through the closed window as if it weren't even there. In the next lightning flash, she saw Gumdrop's worried face gazing up from the comfort of his Kleenex box as she flew past. With a lurch, she felt herself rejoin her body.

She sat up and looked out the window to see if the storm existed here as it did inside her dream. Sure enough, a huge squall was heading straight for the cabin. Karen noticed she was trembling, and pulled the covers up close to her face.

Across the room, Wanda and the other girls in the Turtle cabin were stirring, and one by one flashlights turned on and the girls began talking at once. "I'm scared!" whimpered Gina, as she climbed down out of her top bunk and onto Julie's bed.

The door opened and the light switched on. Sondra walked in, looking very different without her glasses. "It's just a storm, girls," she said in her clear, gentle voice. "You need your sleep, and you'll all be perfectly safe in here. You can watch it if you can't fall asleep right away. It's fun to count the seconds between the flash of lightning and the rumble of thunder. Did you know that every five seconds between the flash and the rumble corresponds to one mile? By counting, you can get an idea of how far away the storm is. Let's get back into our beds and turn off the flashlights, so we can see the lightning better." Sondra's soothing voice was like a magical balm, and even the jumpiest girls returned to their beds, clutching flashlights tightly.

Do you know why we see the flash of lightning before we hear the thunder?" she asked. One of the older girls answered, "Because the speed of light is faster than the speed of sound?"

"That's right!" answered Sondra, "That lightning heats the air around us as much as 55,000 degrees Fahrenheit, which can cook most things it comes in contact with. While the flash of light travels at 186,000 miles per second, the sound waves from the explosion of heated air travel at only 1/5 mile per second."

"Does anyone know why the thunder seems to rumble instead of making one big boom?"

This time, Gina replied. "Is it because the lightning, she is warning us to go inside?"

As all the girls laughed, Sondra said, "Well, let me ask a different question. Do you know what lightning is made of?"

"Light?" suggested Gina.

"No, Fire!" Julie chimed.

"I think it's probably Heat" offered Wanda.

"It's made of electricity!" Sondra told them. It's a good thing we're inside, and that there are lightning rods on top of the cabins because we are fairly safe as long as we stay away from the sink, the shower, and the toilet until the storm is over. Those metal pipes can transmit electricity, and we don't want to feel that much current."

"But I need to go to the bathroom!" squeaked Gina.

"I think you'd better wait, if you can", said Julie, and they exchanged baffled looks.

Sondra continued, "It's a good idea to wait until the storm is over. Lightning can be very unpredictable; we can't tell for sure what it's going to do or where it's going to strike next. Each bolt comes down a little bit at a time in small zigs and zags. There's a negative charge in the clouds that sends out a feeler, which comes down to Earth in a series of invisible steps. When a streamer of positive charge reaches up from the Earth for the negative charge from the cloud, a channel is made, and the visible flash of lightning happens from the ground up to the clouds. Those bolts of lightning are really several short bursts strung together, so many different shock waves happen at different heights above the ground. Since each shock wave comes from a slightly different distance, the thunder seems to rumble."

There was silence for a moment, and then Gina asked, "Wow, Sondra, how did you learn so much about the thunder and lightning?" Her muffled voice came from under her covers.

"I took a meteorology class in college," replied Sondra, pulling her hair back into a ponytail. "I learned a lot about weather there!"

Sondra left the girls to count out loud the seconds between the flashes of lightning and rumbles of thunder. Karen was wondering if she dared fall asleep again after that last dream. Had her dream created this storm, or was the storm already happening and her dream-self just observed it? Sondra's description of zigzag lightning bolts reminded Karen of the markings on the rock. She'd just finished tracing the markings that looked like steps with her fingers when the ferocious storm had begun.

"Pillow fight!" Miranda shouted as she threw her pillow very hard directly at Karen, hitting her in the face. Karen tossed it back in her direction, but it only got as far as Gina's bunk. "Come on… throw it back!" Miranda called, as Gina half-heartedly poked her head up and from under her covers. She tossed it at Heather, who flung it at Wanda.

"Hey! You hit me!" squealed Wanda, before flinging both pillows back at Miranda. Soon, all the girls were tossing pillows at one another and giggling, happy to have found a diversion from worrying about getting struck by lightning.

Karen leaned back on her pillow to watch the lightning and time the seconds between the bright flashes and the low rumbles of thunder. The gap had been between two and three seconds, but now was almost nothing. The storm was at its peak, directly overhead!

Karen jumped when the entire sky flashed white with lightning and the ground shook as a mighty "BOOM!" reverberated through the cabin.

"THAT was a close one!" Julie gasped, as Gina screamed and dove under her covers.

Karen looked at Gumdrop nestled in his Kleenex box and felt proud of how brave such a small rat could be. "It's going to be all right," she told him, and suddenly found herself wishing that someone would offer her such reassurance. After an hour or so, the lightning and thunder moved away, and Karen fell asleep, lulled by the sound of rain hitting the windows.

Halfway between waking and dreaming, Karen saw the woman in white smiling and walking toward her, shining as if lit from within with the brightest light.

Karen was delighted to see her. "You're the woman from my dreams," she exclaimed, "the one with the stone tablet who answers my questions!"

"I am, indeed," the woman replied. "You made a wish to know what is really true, and you made it with all your heart. This means you are ready to begin to awaken within this dream." She paused to gaze directly into Karen's eyes and stroked her hair with her gentle hands before continuing.

"Look carefully around you, and notice anyone who is awake within this dream called life."

"What about you? Will I see you again?"

"Yes, my child!" the woman in white replied as she wrapped Karen in a hug that felt as warm and comfortable as the softest blanket. "You are in my mind and heart always, which means nothing can separate us. You're about to discover that you are always surrounded by love."

With that, the woman disappeared, leaving Karen feeling like she was still wrapped in the warmest love she had ever imagined. That wonderful feeling lasted all the rest of the night, giving Karen a tingling sensation in every cell in her body. When she arose and stretched the next morning, she was glad to see Gumdrop yawn and sneeze in the early morning sunlight.

Karen was glad to be snuggled in such warm blankets. She also felt fortunate to have met Wanda and grateful for the angelic woman of light.

Karen noticed that no one else in the cabin was awake. Gina had climbed down onto Julie's bed and was now snoring softly at Julie's feet with her head under a pillow and her bottom sticking up in the air. Karen turned to look at Wanda and saw she was still gripping her flashlight tightly with the covers next to her chin. Karen grinned at the sight of her friends in such humorous poses, but managed to suppress a laugh. She wanted to go outside and stretch her legs before anyone else woke up and broke the spell of this enchanted moment, so she dressed quickly and silently crept out of the cabin.

Songbirds were chirping all around. Karen smiled at the sheer beauty of this tree-lined camp by the lake and enjoyed the feeling of breathing in the crisp, clear air. The storm had washed everything clean, leaving the trees a brighter shade of green and the ground smelling earthy and fresh.

I wonder what the woman of light meant when she said there are those who are awake within the dream? mused Karen as she walked along the shore of the lake. *How am I supposed to find them, or will they know how to find me?* She looked up and saw a thin wisp of smoke emerging from the chimney of the cabin behind the mess hall and, on impulse, began walking in that direction.

"Certainly if this waking life is a dream and

there are people awake within it who know about this, then someone would have told me before," she said softly to herself. Karen noticed that her words sounded hollow, so she thought they were probably not true. *Is my waking life really a dream? And how can I tell if someone is awake within it?*

Karen continued traveling where her feet took her, enjoying the feeling of the moist earth of the trail on her bare feet. Wet leaves shone on the trees like sparkling jewels in the early morning sunshine. She noticed with a start that she was walking directly up to a man and woman who were standing in front of a little cabin behind the mess hall. They smiled at her, as if they'd been expecting her all along.

"Your feet are wisely walking as your mind and mouth are talking," said the man, before adding, "Glad to meet you! My name is Gill, like the lungs on a fish."

"We're both glad to meet you!" laughed the short, stocky woman standing next to him. "Don't mind Gill. He says whatever comes to his mind, and sometimes it can catch you a bit off-guard! My name is Charlotte Shortgrass. Welcome!" She grinned broadly and stepped forward to give Karen a hug. "We're so glad to see you. Come on inside, and let's have some breakfast, shall we?"

Spider Woman's Web

As Gill and Charlotte busied themselves serving a simple breakfast of tea, fruit and biscuits on the little kitchen table in their cabin, Karen felt overwhelmed with the sense that she was home in a way she'd never been before. It had nothing to do with appearances, for the Shortgrasses were short and stocky and had dark, straight hair and dark brown skin. They did not resemble Karen's family in the least. The feeling of being home came from the way that Gill and Charlotte seemed to know Karen and she felt she knew them, even though they had just met. Recognition and love shone in their eyes and in everything they did. Together, they were a team in mind, body, and spirit. Each seemed to know what the other was doing or thinking. If anyone were to point this out to them, they might have replied, "We are here," and if pressed they would have explained they meant, "We are glad each day to wake up and see the rising sun." Their quiet appreciation for nature's beauty was evident in their every movement and in the tone of their voices when they spoke.

The Shortgrass cabin was built like a miniature house, complete with a combination kitchen / dining room, a bedroom, and a bathroom. It positively glowed with the warm, happy feeling of relaxed and loving inspiration.

Breakfast with the Shortgrasses was an entirely different affair than at the Kimball's. While a meal at the Kimball's usually felt tense and hurried, Karen was refreshed by the way Gill and Charlotte ate breakfast with a feeling of reverent gratitude. Their dining table was adorned with a vase of wildflowers gathered from around the lake, and they frequently looked up to gaze into each other's eyes and smile.

Karen was immediately struck by the beauty of a woven blanked draped over one of the chairs in the Shortgrass cabin. She ran her fingers gently across it.

"Do you like that blanket?" Charlotte asked. "My Navajo grandmother made it herself, with help from her sisters. The design is original. She found the pattern by blowing corn pollen from the palm of her hand onto a spider web and watching what patterns appeared when the pollen stuck to the sticky strands of the web."

"It's very beautiful," Karen replied. "Are you Navajo?"

"Only one quarter. My grandmother left her people when she was a young woman and married a man from outside the Navajo nation, which was quite a scandal in those days."

Karen turned to Gill and asked, "Are you part Navajo, too?"

Gill pointed down to his bare feet and said, "No, I'm part Blackfoot." Karen stared at Gill's feet, feeling confused.

"Oh, Gill!" Charlotte laughed, and then lowered her voice to explain, "He really is part Blackfoot, but you wont' see it by looking at his feet. That's one of the many things I adore about Gill besides his playful sense of humor. We may not always see eye-to-eye, but we both know how it feels to be an outsider." Gill winked at Karen, and began putting on his shoes.

"Well, it's time to roll up our sleeves and get to work cooking breakfast for the rest of the camp," Charlotte announced. "Would you like to come with us? You're welcome in the mess hall as long as you wash your hands and follow our directions." Karen nodded, and watched Charlotte and Gill clear their small dining table of dishes. She gladly joined them as they walked the short distance to the mess hall kitchen, and found herself wondering how Gill and Charlotte could be working at the swim camp as cooking staff without anybody else noticing how special they were.

As if she'd read Karen's mind, Charlotte broke the silence by asking a question, "Have you ever wondered if your father's boss knows who he really is?" Charlotte's eyes twinkled as she put her apron on and washed her hands. "I mean, if your father's boss were to talk to you and find out how your father behaves at home, do you think he would want your father to keep working for him?"

Karen smiled at the thought. She'd never even met her father's boss and she couldn't imagine anyone being thrilled with the way her father behaved at home. Karen watched the Shortgrasses move around the kitchen as if performing a dance they had done many times. "Feel like cracking some eggs?" asked Charlotte, as she placed a large bowl and four dozen eggs on the counter. Karen nodded. Helping made her feel like she belonged. As she took the first egg from the carton and cracked it into the bowl, she considered Charlotte's earlier question. "My dad yells at my brothers and me almost every day. I'm sure he would come up with some reason to explain why he needs to do this, but I don't think anyone would believe it."

"So you don't think your father's boss really knows who he is."

"Right. I guess most grown-ups don't know who other people really are."

"Sleepwalkers!" exclaimed Gill so suddenly that Karen jumped.

"Why do you call them sleepwalkers?" she asked, squinting up at him to see his full reaction to the question.

"Because most of them don't even understand the simple fact that nobody ever dies, for example," said Gill, turning his attention back to the pancake batter he was preparing.

"If people don't die, where do they go when they... die?" asked Karen, her eyes wide with concern.

Gill paused, and studied Karen's face carefully, as if he were deciding whether to tell her something extraordinary. His eyes shone with a firm resolve that indicated he'd chosen to share it.

"Everywhere," said Gill, looking out at the blue sky through the window. Gill's gaze returned to Karen, and he continued. "They return to where they came from before they were born. Sometimes, people awaken within this earthly dream and realize how each of us changes the dream even as we live within it.

Each thought, every feeling has the power to change the world."

"Let me tell you a story about Grandmother Spider Woman," Gill said as he pulled up a chair close to Karen and sat down facing her. He gave Charlotte a questioning look, to which she responded with a nod and a smile, as she took the bowl of batter he'd been mixing and poured some of it onto the hot skillet. He paused for another moment before beginning.

"Once upon a time, the people had a problem with remembering to be grateful. They did not wake up every morning feeling glad to see the sun and the Earth, but instead awakened feeling angry that they had not gotten as much rain as they wanted or that some of their plants were withering or feeling jealous that their neighbors had more good things than they did. The people forgot to greet each other with love and joy. Instead, they blamed one another for causing trouble. Spider Woman watched all this from her quiet web and saw that the people needed a reminder to be thankful again. She came up out of her quiet home in the Earth and tickled the foot of a little boy who was sitting by a stream.

"'Little boy,' said Spider Woman in her soft, silky voice, 'What is it that you need the most?'

"The boy was startled to be awakened by Spider Woman, and he did not know what to say. He started to say that he needed some fish, but then he realized that he was not very hungry. 'I need a new hunting spear,' the boy replied, and Spider Woman nodded.

"'And when you have your hunting spear, you will be happy?' inquired Spider Woman.

"'I will have a hunting spear so I can catch all the fish I can eat!' said the boy. 'Then I can feed all the people, and they will know I am a man.'

"'And then you will be glad?' asked Spider Woman again.

"'I think so,' nodded the boy.

"'How will you feel if you see another boy who has a spear that is sharper and more beautiful than yours?'

"'I will feel sad, and I will need a better spear,' replied the boy.

"'How will you know when your spear is so good that you won't need another?'

"The boy looked at Spider Woman and had no words. Suddenly he said, 'If I had the sharpest, longest, handsomest, strongest, straightest spear there was, then I would be happy.'

"Spider Woman prompted, 'And how would you know yours was best?'

"'Because I would compare mine to all the others and make sure nobody else had a better spear than I.'

"Spider Woman sighed. 'Come with me,' she said, and she led the boy to the people, who gathered in a large circle around them. Spider Woman then announced, 'There is a sickness among us. The people are not happy with what they have, but constantly long for what they do not have. It is time to remember to appreciate who and what is here before everything is gone. It is not too late. While you are still among the wise ones who swim, who walk on four legs, who fly, and who crawl, you can remember to honor the Earth, the air, the water and fire and the four sacred directions. When you feel grateful that you two-legged ones are part of all this, and you show your appreciation to the four directions, the four elements, the four kinds of animals, and the four kinds of plants then you will know that it is not too late.'

"'I will teach you a song to sing so you may know this for all time. When you sing it, be sure to sing it four times.' Then Spider Woman sang."

Karen listened in awe as Gill's deep voice filled the kitchen.

I turn to the Earth in the North.
I bow to those who walk, and plants within the Earth.
Together we stand tall.
I turn to the Air in the East.
I bow to those who fly, and plants that touch the sky.
Together we are free.
I turn to the Fire in the South.
I bow to those who crawl and the desert plants of heat.
Together we burn brightly as the sun.
I turn to the Water in the West.
I bow to those who swim, and the water plants that live therein.
Together we flow as one.

"Spider Woman left the people with instructions to practice the song until they knew it by heart," he continued. "'We have been causing our own problems,' they said, 'but Spider Woman is wise and has shown us that it is not too late.'

"Spider Woman smiled as she looked on from her web and wove a bit more of this dream."

There was silence again as Gill's story came to an end. When Karen looked over at Gill and met his eyes, he asked, "How do you feel after hearing that story?"

"I love the story," Karen replied with a tone of reverence.

Charlotte winked at her from where she was washing strawberries at the sink.

"What happened next? Did the people listen to what Spider Woman said?"

Gill turned to look out the window again, and Karen felt his sorrow. He sighed heavily and replied, "Some people remembered Grandmother Spider Woman's song, but many forgot. If you look around at the people now, you will see few who revere the Earth and animals as we do."

Gill turned back to face Karen and continued, "There is wisdom, love, and life in everything. Even the stones are conscious."

"How can you tell?" Karen asked, "I mean, sometimes I've thought I've thought I heard my pet rat talking to me. Can all plants and animals talk to us?"

"Shut your eyes and make your mind very still, and you will see more clearly," Gill responded. "When you learn to listen and see what is truly real, you will hear and see much more than your senses tell you."

For a fleeting moment, Karen imagined that she was back in kindergarten, and it was show and tell time. She smiled at the idea of asking the five-year-old children to close their eyes, quiet their minds, and see more clearly. Some of them would wriggle and squirm and peek through the fingers covering their eyes, and others would giggle. Still, they might be able to sense much more, simply because they hadn't yet been told such things weren't possible.

A whistle sounded from inside the dining room of the mess hall, and Karen leaped off her chair exclaiming, "Thanks so much for everything! I've got to go now. It's time to line up for breakfast!"

Swimming Turtles

As she joined the breakfast line, Karen contemplated Gill's story about Spider Woman. She could feel the truth in his words, yet needed time to absorb their meaning.

"THERE you are!" shouted Wanda, running up to Karen, grabbing her arms and swinging her around and around. "I thought you'd washed away in the storm!"

"I woke up early and went for a walk," Karen replied, leaving out the part about meeting Gill and Charlotte. It was too hard to explain everything that was happening, especially when she was still trying to figure it out herself.

"DING! DING! DING!" rang the clear tones of a water glass being struck by a table knife. Mike stood atop one of the benches. "May I have your attention please! I wish to announce on behalf of our lovely camp director, ChaCha, that we will be having daily swim races to help you develop your skills. The races will be held at 2:00 every afternoon of swim camp. Each team is depending on its members to do their best, so at the end of camp you can bring home a trophy!"

The room buzzed excitement, and once again Mike's water glass chimed. "QUIET, Please! Our four swim instructors and ChaCha herself will judge this contest, so it is important that you all do your very best. Today's race will be a relay, where all members of your team will get a chance to swim. Your instructors will tell you more when you go out to the lake after breakfast."

Karen did not share the excitement of many of the campers. She felt nervous because she had only just begun to learn to swim yesterday, and so far was not even very competent at the dog paddle. She didn't want to embarrass herself and her team by dragging up the rear, and wished she could find some way out of it. She turned her fork end over end as she contemplated her predicament.

"It's all right," said Wanda, sensing what was on Karen's mind. "They must know that some of us can't swim, and I'm sure we've been assigned to the cabins fairly, so there are good swimmers on each team."

"I just wish I didn't have to race," said Karen. "I just know I must be the slowest swimmer here."

"It's OK. You'll get better the more you practice!" beamed Wanda. Karen was happy to hear her words, even if she couldn't yet feel the truth of them. She stopped fiddling with her fork and said aloud, "I'll get better the more I practice." Wanda's words had the ring of truth, and she smiled back broadly. "You know what? I think you're RIGHT!"

A boy with dark unkempt hair walked over to their table, interrupting their happy moment. He said in a low, menacing voice, "So you think you have a chance of winning, huh? The TURTLES? What a laugh! They've never won a championship at this camp, and they never will. You're going to have to face it. The Flying Fish always win!" Before any of the Turtles had a chance to respond, he sidled off wearing a sneer of contempt.

"Who is that?" asked Karen to no one in particular, "and what's his problem?" Behind her, a girl's voice replied, "Kirk Dempsey. He's on the Flying Fish team, and he's been coming here to swim camp every summer for years. He thinks he owns the place."

Karen looked up to see a smiling brunette with long, straight hair. "My name's Rhonda, and I'm in the River Otters. Last summer our team really was the fastest, but the Flying Fish won the Lovell Cup in the end-of-camp race. It was bad enough to lose, but even worse to hear Kirk gloating about it."

"That's terrible!" Karen agreed.

Jasper clapped her hands and called out, "River Otters! It's our time to shine!" She tossed her head so her bangle earrings jangled, and playfully stuck her tongue out at Mike as the procession of River Otters filed out the door behind her. "Beat you there," she challenged him as she and the Otters broke into a run. "Bye! See you at the lake!" Rhonda called back to Karen.

"Hey!" shouted Mike as he scrambled to assemble his team of Water Snakes. Karen watched Ben and the other Water Snakes hastily form a ragged line by the door before following Jasper and her team of River Otters to the lake.

Kirk was now standing alongside the other Flying Fish, and Karen noticed that they were all dressed in various shades of blue and black. They leaned against the wall by the mess hall door with their arms crossed. Karen noted that their swim instructor, Steve, was nowhere to be seen, and Sondra had already left the mess hall.

ChaCha blew her whistle and waved her arms in a grand sweeping gesture to the mess hall door, signaling that breakfast was over and it was time to suit up and head for the lake. The Flying Fish were still standing by the door as Karen and Wanda walked past. Kirk could be heard loudly whispering to his buddies, "There go the Turdles – watch out that you don't step on one!" The other boys snickered, and Karen shot Kirk a look of contempt. She was beginning to understand why Andy had gone silent the night before when the Flying Fish joined the dinner line.

"If you knew what you sounded like, you'd worry about something else entirely," Karen said to Kirk as she and the other Turtles left the hall.

"If you knew what you were getting into, you'd prepare yourself," Kirk shouted after her. "There's something evil at the bottom of the lake that's been trapped there for centuries, and one day it's going to escape and get you!"

Karen shook her head in disgust and walked on. Although she tried not to show it, Kirk's words troubled her. If there really was something evil at the bottom of the lake, she needed to find out what it was and whether there was anything she could do. She wanted to ask Gill and Charlotte about it, but there was no time for that now.

Sondra greeted the Turtles by the lake, and Karen noted that as usual, the older more experienced Turtles had arrived at the lake first. "We're going to practice swimming the relay race this morning, so you'll get used to it,"

Sondra said as she brushed her long hair out of her face. "That way, it won't seem so scary when you're competing this afternoon. Swim out to the raft, and then tag your partner who will swim back this way. Keep tagging partners until everyone has had a chance to swim."

"Aren't we supposed to wait for thirty minutes after eating before we go swimming so that we don't cramp up or drown?" Julie asked.

"No, that's just an old wives tale," Sondra briskly replied, as she motioned for the girls to enter the water.

The more Karen tried to coordinate her arms and legs, the more hopeless it seemed. Although her fellow Turtles were kind as they watched her struggle to perfect her technique, she felt like she didn't belong in the group. When Miranda gave her a condescending look, Karen felt even worse. "Try to think like the dog," suggested Gina.

"Pretend your hands and feet are webbed like a duck," said Wanda.

"Or just imagine you are being chased by a shark," offered Julie, putting her hands together like a shark fin on top of her head.

It didn't matter what she tried, Karen couldn't seem to get coordinated.

"You're doing fine," Sondra told her, but Karen could tell she was just being nice.

"The truth is that even CATS can dog paddle better than I can," said Karen dejectedly as she flopped down on the sand next to Wanda after her practice run. "I could hardly do worse if I were trying to swim backwards."

Julie wailed in the background, "I think I'm cramping up! My side hurts!"

"Hey, maybe that's it! You've been thinking

you're so terrible that it's making you swim terribly!" exclaimed Wanda. "All you need to do is say that you're the fastest swimmer in the lake, and then see what happens!"

Karen stared at Wanda for a moment, watching the beautiful yellow and pink colors that so often shone around her shoulders and head when she was especially happy. "What have I got to lose? I can't think of anything better to try," Karen agreed. It's kind of embarrassing to say that kind of thing out loud, though."

"Just shut your eyes and whisper to yourself: 'I'm the fastest swimmer at Lovell Lake.' Keep saying it until you start to believe it might be true. Say it softly so just you and I can hear it. You know I won't make fun of you."

Karen gave Wanda one long probing look before whispering, "I'm the fastest swimmer at Lovell Lake. I'm the fastest swimmer at Lovell Lake. I'm the fastest swimmer at Lovell Lake." She felt more confident and sensed that this feeling could help her do anything better. "You know what, Wanda?" Karen smiled. "I think you're right. I think this helps!"

Wanda beamed back her brightest smile and clapped her hands with delight. "I know it helps, and I know you'll do just great!"

ChaCha's whistle blew, telling the campers that the morning swim session was over and it was time to go eat lunch. Karen sighed, realizing she hadn't had much of a chance to swim after Wanda's wonderful suggestion. Lunch was a simple meal of burritos and rice, but Karen saw Gill wink at her with love when he handed her plate over, and she caught Charlotte smiling at her from the kitchen. Karen loved the idea that she had such good friends hiding in full view! They were right in plain sight for everyone to see, but she seemed to be the only one who truly saw them.

There wasn't much time after lunch to prepare for the race, so Karen used every spare minute to repeat her new mantra, "I'm the fastest swimmer at Lovell Lake." She was careful to say it quietly enough that only Wanda could hear. A tingling pulse ran through her whole body, as if she were being tickled with happy energy.

As Karen floated in the lake prior to the race, she closed her eyes and tried to remember Spider Woman's song. The song mentioned something about four directions, four elements, and four kinds of plants and animals, but she couldn't quite remember what. She felt something brush past her leg under the water, and opened her eyes with a start to see a real turtle swimming in the water alongside her! It's short legs paddled slowly but surely, moving it along at a steady pace.

Karen felt a rush of love for this wild creature. If she hadn't seen him, she would never have known that something so awkward-looking could be such an elegant swimmer. She turned to tap Wanda softly on her shoulder. "Look," she pointed, "I think this is a good sign."

Wanda gasped at the sight of the little brown turtle. "That's for sure!" she chirped. "We found our mascot!"

"The amazing thing," Karen told her "is I had shut my eyes and was thinking about animal wisdom when that turtle bumped right into me.

And it's the same animal that our swim team is named after!"

"I'm SO glad that we're not in the Water Snakes!" laughed Wanda.

The afternoon swim was filled with a buzz of excitement as all the teams gathered together around ChaCha. Her golden one-piece swimsuit was so shiny that it was hard to look directly at her as she announced, "Today is the first of our afternoon races. Each team will compete, and I will keep track of your finish times. By the end of swim camp, I'm counting on all of you to improve your times. I'll post your scores on the office bulletin board after each race."

The four teams split into two groups, half of them swimming out to the raft in the middle of lake and the other half staying back on shore. Each team had a different colored bracelet to carry as their "torch" to pass. The Turtles had a purple bracelet, the Water Snakes a green one, the Flying Fish had blue, and the River Otters had a red bracelet.

ChaCha blew her whistle again, and said, "Starter swimmers, get on your marks." Then, "Get set. GO!"

The four fastest swimmers from each team went first. They employed a variety of strokes – Flying Fish's swimmer was using a butterfly to good advantage, while the Water Snakes swimmer was doing the Australian crawl. The River Otters' starter swimmer was surprisingly fast at the backstroke, and the Turtles lead swimmer, Miranda Garrett, was in the lead also with a butterfly stroke.

Karen could hardly believe the speed with which these swimmers moved through the water. She couldn't help comparing her floundering to their powerful strokes, but stopped and remembered to repeat her mantra a few more times for good measure. Her heart pounded as she moved forward and watched Turtles passing the purple bracelet and swimming to the raft and back.

There were two girls ahead of her... then just one... and finally it was her turn! She saw Gina coming towards her, splashing a lot and gulping for air as she flailed her arms in her best effort to "do the Australian crawl without drowning."

Karen grasped the bracelet and quickly put it on her arm so she could concentrate on the only stroke she knew – the dog paddle. She jumped into the water and was off like a shot. For the first time, she felt her arms and legs moving in unison. She was moving fast! Encouraged, she made bigger, stronger kicks and took bigger strokes with her arms. She looked over to the next team, and couldn't tell whether she was ahead or behind, so she looked back to the raft where Wanda was waiting for her. Waves came up and splashed her face, but Karen didn't mind. She was going to make it!

"Excellent!" exclaimed Wanda, pulling the bracelet off Karen's wrist and slipping it onto her arm before taking off with a splash.

Karen gasped for breath and realized with a sense of growing pride that she'd done it. She'd swum the fastest dog paddle she could! She clung to the raft and watched Wanda splashing her way across the lake to the shore. As Wanda swam, the splashing decreased somewhat and her strokes became more efficient. Karen was proud to see that it looked like Wanda was also going faster with each determined kick.

As the last swimmer came in, ChaCha blew her whistle and announced, "Well done, campers! Today's champions are the Flying Fish, followed by the River Otters, the Turtles, and the Water Snakes. You'll all get a chance tomorrow to better your scores, so keep practicing!"

Karen glanced over at the Flying Fish and sensed something was wrong, but couldn't quite determine what it was. Kirk was smirking at her, with a look that seemed to say, "You'll never be able to do what we can do." Just then, Julie ran over. "We DID it!" she bubbled. "We came in third! With a bit more practice, we can win the trophy!"

Julie turned her head to see what Karen was staring at. Kirk had begun to chant in a low voice:

"Flying Fish are the best
for succeeding at any test.
We're faster and stronger than all the rest!"

His face shone with fierce determination as he finished the chant, and many of the Flying Fish leaped into the air and whooped. Several boys snapped their wet towels at each other. Kirk snapped his towel at ChaCha just as she walked by. She stopped and gave him a quizzical look, then commented loudly so all could hear, "It looks like someone needs a kiss!"

Children from all four teams laughed and exclaimed, "Whoo-hoo!" as ChaCha leaned closer and closer to Kirk and gave him a loving smooch on his left cheek, leaving a big pink lipstick mark. Kirk immediately tried to wipe the lipstick off, but it stubbornly remained in place, as his whole face flushed to match its shade.

"Oh my gosh! Did you see THAT?!" Julie exclaimed, "Kirk's wearing lipstick! I may die laughing!"

"You'd better not – we need you alive so we still have a chance to win," said Gina in a mock stern voice.

Karen and Wanda smiled at each other and then broke out in laughter. Karen looked over at Kirk to see him licking his hands and rubbing his face, still trying to remove the lipstick. Karen's eyes twinkled as she said, "I know one boy who won't skip his shower tonight!"

The Biggest Promise

Karen walked back to the cabin with Wanda and the other Turtles, wondering how she could get some more time with Gill and Charlotte before dinner.

"I need to help out in the kitchen tonight," she told Wanda, "so I'll be going directly to the mess hall after I shower. I'll meet you there, okay?"

"Did you get in trouble? What's wrong? You can tell me!" squealed Wanda in a plaintive whine.

"No, it's nothing like that. I just promised the kitchen staff that if they needed any help, I'd pitch in." Karen's face and neck flushed hot at this white lie. She hadn't actually made any such promise, but she felt she needed an excuse to talk to Gill and Charlotte again.

Wanda pouted at Karen. She sat on her lower bunk, fire burning in her green eyes. "Well, a promise is a promise, so you'd better keep your word," was all she said. Her tone was icy, and Karen felt terrible. She wished she could think of some way to let Wanda know the real reason she wanted to go to the mess hall, but it didn't feel right just yet.

Karen glanced over to see Gumdrop standing at the door of his cage looking as brave and determined as a rat can be, with his softly trembling whiskers and brightly shining eyes. She felt encouraged to see him at his door like that. He seemed to be letting her know that he understood, and that it was okay for her to just go! She opened the cage and gave him a peanut. "Bye, Gumdrop!" whispered Karen, "I love you! I'll play with you before I go to bed tonight."

"Humph", snorted Wanda. Her arms were still crossed and her mouth was still turned downwards.

Karen showered and changed in record time, then sprinted down the wooded path to the mess hall with mixed feelings about having left Wanda behind. Each fluid stride was longer than the one before, and about every tenth step she felt both of her feet were in the air. Running made Karen feel better, as she left her guilty feelings behind with every step. She was lighter and springing up higher with every bound. She was flying! Karen arrived at the mess hall feeling buoyant and radiant. When she entered the open door to the mess hall, she found Gill and Charlotte in the kitchen chopping vegetables. Charlotte looked up and smiled. Without a word, she handed Karen an apron, as if she'd been expecting her.

"What can I do to help?" Karen asked, going to the sink to wash her hands.

Charlotte brought a large bowl of carrots over to the sink. "You'd be a dear to peel these carrots! she beamed."

Karen smiled back, and then broke out in goose bumps when she glanced out the window and saw two enormous eyes looking in at her. It was a large stag! His huge head supported antlers that each had three points. Karen stood open-mouthed in wonder for several seconds. When she caught her breath, she whispered, "There's a deer at the window!" She continued to gaze deeply into the stag's dark, dewy eyes.

"Yes, you're a dear to help peel those carrots!" Charlotte replied, smiling and not even looking up from her work at the cutting board.

"No, I mean there's a   *real* deer! Karen continued gazing at the stag, which stood perfectly still, except for occasional twitching of his ears at flies. Karen felt a sense of deep trust as she looked into the dark eyes, and she longed to somehow tell him how beautiful he was to her.

"Things like that often happen when you begin to awaken within this dream. Something you say appears moments after you say it. This is why it's so important to only say what you want to come true." Charlotte looked up at the window and added, "That stag comes here at dinner time sometimes. If you like, you can bring him the carrot peelings. He is a wild animal in body, but he has a gentle spirit inside."

"I think I know what you mean! I saw a beautiful wild turtle swimming in the lake this afternoon. He bumped into me right after I'd shut my eyes and was thinking about animal wisdom!"

"You are connected to all that is, and you can start to see that the spirit in all that is talks to you through everything around you," Charlotte replied.

Karen worked quickly to make a big pile of carrot peelings to bring to the stag. "I told my friend I'd promised to help you because I want to ask you some questions about the waking dream and some evil thing a boy thinks is living at the bottom of the lake. I told Wanda I'd promised to help you whenever I had a spare minute, but since I never said that to you, I feel like I lied to her."

Charlotte and Gill listened in silence as they continued chopping zucchini, tomatoes, and onions in a musical rhythm.

"So I ran over here and wanted to let you know that I'd like to make that true. If it's OK with you, I'd like to come help you out every chance I get!"

Charlotte met Karen's intense gaze and said, "That's the biggest promise there is, offering something in words that your heart has already given. Of course, we know you love to be with us, and I hope you know you and your friends are always welcome here!"

Charlotte hugged Karen close for several seconds, then stepped back to look deeply into her eyes. "For such a young girl, you sometimes surprise people by showing the heart of an ancient one!" Karen turned to look out the window at the stag, and pondered what that meant.

From the other side of the kitchen, Gill asked, "Who told you about something evil at the bottom of the lake?"

"Kirk Dempsey. He said that it has been trapped there for centuries and that one day it's going to escape. Is that really true?"

Gill sighed, and set down his knife. "Yes and no. As with most tales told by sleepwalkers, he got the facts right and the feelings wrong. The feelings are the key to comprehending this universe, so until you get the right key, you can't

unlock the secrets hidden right in front of you."
Karen listened quietly, not knowing what to ask
to encourage Gill to say more.

"The less people understand about a thing,
the more they read their own fears and desires
into it. Since Kirk does not know the true nature
of the thing at the bottom of the lake, he can only
describe it as he would imagine his own inner
demons and angels."

"So it's not an evil thing that's out to get
me?" asked Karen, setting her carrot down so
she wouldn't accidentally cut herself with the
peeler.

"What do you think?" asked Gill, his eyes
dancing with some inner delight. He seemed
confident that Karen would be able to sense
what Kirk could not.

"I don't know," said Karen, feeling flustered,
"I haven't taken the time to talk to it, and I don't
know how to go about doing that."

"I trust that if you wish to, you will find a
way," Gill said supportively.

Karen thought for several quiet moments
about the spirits she had talked to. Some were
very helpful and had offered exactly the advice
she needed when she needed it, while others had
scared her. She looked up at Gill. "I know that
some spirits really are evil because there is one
in particular who keeps bothering me," she
confided.

Gill's eyes burned with a look of intense
fascination. They seemed to say, "Go on, " so
Karen continued.

"The first time I met him, he wanted to make
a deal with me. He said I could be as smart as
my brothers."

"What did you do?" asked Charlotte, who was now also watching Karen with total concentration.

"I said 'No' that I didn't accept his offer"

"And what did he do?"

"Nothing at first. But he came back last night during that big thunderstorm. I was flying around over the cabin in a dream, and he told me to 'Go away!'"

"And?" pressed Charlotte.

Seeing that both Charlotte and Gill were taking her seriously gave Karen confidence to continue. "Well, he told me he's been waiting for me for a long time, and that some day I'll summon him. I flew back inside my sleeping body, and woke up to see the storm I'd been dreaming about was real. Before I left, he touched me and it felt like a real touch. And I asked his name and he told me it was Ohgeenay."

"Ohgeenay!" exclaimed Charlotte, with a knowing smile.

Gill wasn't smiling, but some of his tension seemed to dissipate. Karen sensed from their reactions that they might have already met this spirit. "Do you know him?" she asked.

"In a way," Charlotte replied, returning to her work. "His name means 'the one who tests us by bringing to us all that we doubt in ourselves and all that we most fear.' We know Ohgeenay through the people of the Cree nation as that which afflicts us when we have done something wrong. Conscience, in other words."

"How can I make him go away?"

"You'll have to face and overcome all of your deepest fears and doubts. There is no quick and easy way to dismiss him."

Karen was quiet for several minutes before speaking again. "I also have a question about the markings on a boulder on the far side of the lake. I saw two dots that look like eyes, next to a circle inside a bigger circle, and to the right of those were markings that look like steps. Do you know what they mean?"

"You already know more than your realize," grinned Gill, picking up his knife and resuming his chopping of the vegetables. "Those markings have been etched in stone since before my grandfather's grandfather's days on Earth, and are some of the oldest writings known to man. They speak only to those who listen, and teach those who are willing to learn."

Karen felt a heightened awareness of everything around her as if she had feelers extending several feet out from her body. She'd had goose bumps on her skin as she'd described her encounters with Ohgeenay, the spirit at the bottom of the lake, and the rock markings. She sighed, sensing that this was going to be a mystery she'd have to solve herself. She scooped up her carrot peelings and carried them to the stag at the door, which gently nibbled right out of her hands! She smiled to feel the warm velvet of his lips touching her palms and his hot breath blowing softly on her skin. She kept a watchful eye on his antlers as his head bobbed slightly up and down as he ate.

Trapped

Dinner that evening was a delicious vegetable stew that Karen felt proud to have helped make by adding the peeled carrots. She helped Gill and Charlotte set out the bowls and silverware, still steaming hot from the dishwasher and then joined the line forming in the mess hall. Karen was glad that even though Wanda still seemed sulky, she came to stand next to her in line.

"I didn't mean to run away from you," Karen started to explain, "It's just that I promised Gill and Charlotte that I'd help them in the kitchen."

Wanda stood silently looking down at her shoes.

"I'll make it up to you, though. If you want, you can come with me this evening after dinner to see whether Kirk's telling the truth about the evil thing trapped at the bottom of the lake. I'm starting to think there might be something to it, and I want to see if I can gather any clues." Wanda's eyes widened with awe as she met Karen's gaze. "You mean it?" she asked. "You're really going to look for it?"

"Yup", said Karen. "All I know so far is that there's a possibility that Kirk is right, that something is trapped at the bottom of the lake. I need to find out what else he knows before doing some of my own investigation."

"You're really planning to go to the lake at night? I wouldn't do that if someone paid me a million dollars!"

Karen shuffled her feet and reached for her bowl of vegetable stew and corn bread, winking and smiling back at Charlotte as she passed the food to her. As she walked over to where the Turtles sat, Karen paused at the Flying Fish table. She looked at Kirk with a sweet smile and asked, "Who told you about the spirit at the bottom of the lake?" The compassionate way that Karen asked this question caught Kirk by surprise, and he smiled back at her in spite of himself.

"Digger Drummond, the groundskeeper," Kirk replied. "He said that when he's gone out to the lake at night, he's heard an eerie wailing sound like someone crying. He's only heard it a few times, but the groundskeeper before him heard it, too. There's an Indian legend that a medicine man caught an evil spirit and trapped it there."

Kirk then burped loudly, which inspired the other boys at the Flying Fish table to laugh raucously and start an impromptu burping competition. Karen's "thank you" was drowned out by the din. Looking across the table, she caught Andy's eye. He shook his head and pinched his nose shut. Karen smiled at him before turning away, then walked back to join the Turtles.

"Wow, Kirk seems to know a lot about the spirit in the lake," Karen said as she sat down with Wanda at the end of the bench.

"Yeah. He must have gotten to know the groundskeeper like you know the kitchen staff.

So you're really serious about finding what's trapped at the bottom of the lake? How are you going to do that?"

"I don't know yet," Karen replied, lowering her voice. "But I'd rather not talk about it here. If you want, you can meet me down by the lake after dinner, and wear your swimsuit under your clothes."

After dinner, Karen and Wanda walked down to the lake and on past the dock. They sat down on a couple of large boulders, still warm from the day's sun. "So now what do we do?" chirped Wanda. "Are you thinking of swimming to the other side of the lake?"

"We wait... quietly," Karen replied, hoping that Wanda could take a hint, and doing her best to conceal a growing sense of anxiety.

"For how long?" asked Wanda, adjusting her swimsuit straps under her T-shirt.

"Until it gets dark... or we hear something... or feel something...or see or sense something," Karen answered. She felt goose bumps forming on her arms, and was gripped by an uncontrollable urge to shiver.

"I brought something for good luck," Wanda said, pulling a long blue and purple scarf from her pocket. "I got it from my aunt last winter, and it's always made me feel good." Wanda handed it to Karen saying, "Now I want to give it to you."

Karen did not reach out to take the beautiful scarf.

"I have lots of other scarves," Wanda added, noting Karen's hesitation. "My aunt gets them for me almost every time she travels, and she travels a lot. Here, I'll help you put it on."

When Wanda finished tying the scarf as a headband for Karen, she said, "There! Now you're ready for anything!"

"I don't know how to thank you…" Karen began, feeling choked up with emotion. She'd never had anything so lovely.

Wanda interjected, "That's OK. Being my best friend is thanks enough. Besides, I'm wearing my good luck necklace, and you need good luck, too!"

The setting sun had already gone behind the mountains on the far side of the lake, and Karen whispered to Wanda. "Let's swim to the other side. I need to get a closer look at the strange markings on that boulder across the lake."

Wanda's eyes got big as she watched Karen strip down to her swimsuit. "But how will we be able to see anything over there in the dark?" she squeaked.

Karen pulled a flashlight out of the pocket of her shorts, and put it between her teeth. "C'mon!" she murmured, as she began slowly wading into the wet mud at the water's edge.

Wanda hesitated for a moment before removing her clothes and following Karen into the water. "But we're not allowed on the other side," Wanda whispered.

Karen tried to smile reassuringly back at Wanda, but thanks to the flashlight in her mouth, it looked more like a grimace.

The girls stopped to catch their breath when they reached the raft in the middle of the lake. Karen set her flashlight down and whispered to Wanda, "How are you doing? Do you think you can make it all the way across?"

"Well, now that you mention it, I'm thinking

maybe this is as far as we should go. ChaCha told us she had a good reason for staying away from the far side of the lake. It's starting to get really dark, too."

"I feel scared, too," Karen admitted, "but I need you to come with me. It won't take very long."

"But Sondra's going to notice we're missing," Wanda whined. "And what happens if we can't make it back?"

Karen sighed. "Wanda, there's something I haven't told you about."

Fear shone in Wanda's eyes as she whispered almost silently, "What?"

"I've been to the far side of the lake already... in my dreams. These dreams were real, and I know that when we get to the boulder with the markings, we'll find something amazing. I know this is true, because I can feel it."

Wanda gaped at Karen open mouthed for several long moments.

Stars twinkled in the clear night sky, as hundreds of bats performed their nightly ballet, catching flying insects overhead. All around the lake, crickets chirped and frogs croaked. Bats danced down to the shimmering water and touched their wing tips close to the surface in their pursuit of insects, as occasional little bubbles rose from deep at the bottom of the lake.

"OK," whispered Wanda, "Let's go before I change my mind."

Karen reached the far side of the lake first, and almost fell down as soon as she tried to stand up. "Be careful! There are rocks on the bottom, instead of mud, and some of them fall over when you step on them." Karen swept the beach with the beam of her flashlight, and gingerly led Wanda out of the lake and onto dry land at the foot of the boulder.

"Wow! Look at that!" Wanda exclaimed, pointing at the markings on the giant rock. "What do you think they mean?"

"I don't know... but they seem to say something important. These two dots here remind me of eyes. The circle within a circle is very strange, but it seems important. Those zigzag lines on the right look like steps, so maybe there are some steps here that we can see if we look around." Karen shone the flashlight in all directions, but only saw the rocky bush-covered mountainside.

Wanda shivered. "Now what? How do we find that amazing thing?"

Karen sighed. "I don't really know. I hoped it would be obvious."

"Maybe we should go back, then."

"No – wait a minute! I have an idea. You hold the flashlight, and I'll see if I can feel anything unusual as I walk around. I'm going to hold my hands out in front of me and see if I can sense anything that feels different."

Karen stretched her fingers out and immediately felt a tingly sensation in her right hand. "I think I *can* feel something here!" She stepped slowly in the direction her hand was pointing, and the tingling sensation became more noticeable. Now both hands were tingling and Karen continued slowly walking toward a large bush at the foot of the mountain. The tingling was now so intense that Karen exclaimed, "This must be it!"

"What? A bush?!" Wanda giggled, shaking

the flashlight.

"No! Look at this! This bush is hiding something... I see a cave back there!"

"Here," said Wanda, hastily passing the flashlight to Karen. "Do you think it's big enough to climb inside?"

"Let's find out!" whispered Karen, as she brushed a branch aside and got down on hands and knees to peer deep inside the dank recesses of the hole. "I see a long path going up that looks just like steps on a staircase. This must be what the markings mean, 'look around and you'll see a cave near here with steps going up'!"

"Wow!" breathed Wanda as she followed Karen inside the cave and up the stony steps. "Where do you think these steps go? It smells really strange in here. Kind of like the moss on the side of a tree... but more so."

Karen gasped as she reached the top of the steps, and stopped.

"What? I can't see! What are you looking at?" Wanda squealed, hopping up and down to catch a glimpse over Karen's shoulders. The girls entered a chamber the size of Karen's bedroom that was piled high with stacks of boxes marked "Explosives."

"There must be twenty boxes of explosives in here, if these are what they say they are," gasped Wanda.

"I just counted thirty... and every one of them looks like it is what it says it is. All of a sudden I feel like we'd better get out of here."

"I'm with you!" said Wanda, turning around and retreating down the stone steps. "I could use some light over here!"

As the girls exited the cave, Karen asked,

"Who would put all those explosives inside that cave?"

"I have absolutely no idea, but I don't want to tell anyone we were over on the far side of the lake."

"Maybe we can find out. Maybe there really is some kind of spooky noise in the lake at night, and it will help explain what is going on," mused Karen before putting her flashlight back in her mouth for the return swim across the lake to camp.

"I've had about all I can take of spooky for one night," shivered Wanda, as she followed Karen into the cold, dark waters of Lake Lovell.

When the girls reached the camp side of the lake, Karen said, "You'd better go back to camp and cover for me. I need to know if that story is true about something being trapped in the lake."

"Are you sure you'll be OK alone out here?" asked Wanda with an edge of panic in her voice.

"Positive," replied Karen with more confidence than she felt. "If I need help, I know how to yell."

"Come back as soon as you can – and promise you'll tell me if anything happens."
"I promise!" Karen said, waving as Wanda skipped back down the path to her cabin.

After another thirty minutes had passed with nothing unusual happening, Karen gave up and walked back to the cabin. She stretched up onto her tiptoes, sighing softly and snapping a twig under one foot. For a moment, the frogs and crickets stopped their songs. In this moment of sudden quiet, Karen heard what sounded like a muffled cry coming from the center of the lake. She froze. Could this be what she'd been waiting for? Although it was getting quite dark, she could see the surface of the lake clearly. She didn't notice anything that might be making the sound, so she stood very still and tucked her hair back behind her ears to listen more carefully.

There it was again, only longer. This time, it lasted for almost four seconds. It sounded like a coyote's cry, except it was not as clear. Karen realized that if she weren't listening so intently, she probably wouldn't have noticed it. The sound definitely seemed to be coming from the center of the lake!

Digger Drummond

Karen was certain now that there was something out there, but what? How could she find out? Gill said that she'd find a way, and standing alone on the side of the lake where it lived seemed the perfect time to do something, if she could only think what that might be. Standing up to her full height, Karen cleared her throat and said aloud to the lake, "Hello! My name is Karen, and I have come to talk to you!" For the next several minutes, she focused all her attention on listening, but heard nothing. Even the frogs and crickets were still quiet. She tried again. "I have come to find out who you are and how you are doing." She listened more carefully than ever, making sure that even her breathing was silent. Then she heard it! Just above the rustle of the wind in the trees, she was certain she'd heard something saying, "Help me."

"Who are you, and what do you need?" Karen called out.

"Help... me," the soft voice repeated.

Perhaps whoever it was had gone insane after being trapped down at the bottom of the lake or was afraid to tell Karen the truth about how this predicament came about. In any event, it wasn't volunteering much information, and Karen was starting to feel a strong desire to go back to the cabin. She wanted to talk to some regular people again, not just a disembodied voice!

As she began to walk away, the voice again said, "Please help me!" Karen stopped and called back, "First, I need to know who you are and what happened to you." She listened harder than ever, but there was only silence, and a few minutes later the crickets and frogs could again be heard.

As she headed back along the dirt trail, Karen wondered how she was ever going to help someone who wouldn't tell her who they were or what had happened to them. When she reached the cabin, Wanda was lying in bed reading a book. "Tell me all about it!" she whispered excitedly. Karen put her index finger to her lips. "Shh! I don't want to talk about it here. I'll tell you tomorrow morning after breakfast."

"Tell me *now!*" Wanda insisted, climbing out of her bed and walking over to Karen's. Her green eyes were flashing a look of fierce determination as she added, "If you whisper, nobody can hear."

Karen opened Gumdrop's cage to offer him a carrot slice she'd saved from dinner. He bit into one end and carried the over-sized load back to his nesting box, bumping into the side of his cage with a faint "Thump!" as he turned around. Karen smiled. "OK," she said to Wanda, "but there's not much to tell."

The girls sat down on Karen's bed, and Karen related what she had heard. "That's SCARY!" Wanda exclaimed forgetting to whisper.

"Shh!" Karen reminded her. Then she added, "I think tomorrow I should go talk to the groundskeeper."

"I don't want to swim in a haunted lake!" whispered Wanda, "What if it tries to get us when we're swimming?"

"If it could have done that, I'm sure someone would have been gotten by now," said Karen in a voice that sounded more reassuring than she felt. "It must be trapped down there. If what Kirk says is true, it's unable to move or do anything. Besides, I'm more concerned about all those explosives, because if they go off, they could take a lot of the mountain down with them."

"Take me with you tomorrow to see the groundskeeper – PLEASE!" Wanda begged, "I want to help you figure out what's going on!"

"OK, but don't tell anyone else. It won't help if people start panicking about all this." Karen also realized she didn't want an audience watching her attempt to solve a mystery when she didn't have any idea what she was doing. She opened Gumdrop's cage and carried him over to the towel she'd spread out on her bed. He stretched his legs and seemed to enjoy getting a change of scenery. She petted his soft fur and made a tunnel in the towel for him to walk through. Then she gave him another big hug before tucking him back into his Kleenex box. She cleaned out his litter, replacing the used wood shavings with new ones, and refilled his food and water containers. These little tasks helped soothe her nerves and took her mind off Ohgeenay, the cave full of explosives, and the disembodied voice in the lake.

That night, Karen dreamed of glistening dewdrops on a spider web. Each drop of dew shone like a jewel, and when she peered into one she saw a person moving around inside. Looking at the entire web felt like watching a thousand movies at once – and every time she stopped to peer in closer at one particular person she saw many possible scenes being played out. She flew from bead to shining jewel-like bead, seeing the way each person's choices affected every other person in the web. Karen was surprised to see a movie of her own life that showed one possible reality in which she stayed home and read books all summer. In that reality, she made no new friends all summer long. Karen zoomed from one bead to another, flying in close so that she was the same size as the drops of dew, to glimpse as many possible realities as she could.

She was surprised to see Andy inside a shining dew drop bead, lying on his bunk bed with both arms crossed beneath his head. He seemed sad about something, and as the scene repeated itself over and over again, he kept standing up and walking to the bathroom to brush his teeth. The first time he stood up, he walked past Kirk without acknowledging him at all. The second time, Andy made an elaborate show of bowing to Kirk before walking by. There were about a dozen variations on different ways Andy greeted or ignored Kirk altogether, and Karen watched in rapt fascination that such a seemingly insignificant interaction could be so carefully choreographed.

The woman in white asked Karen, "What do you see when you look at this web?"

Karen answered, "I see people doing things many different ways."

The woman replied, "This is the web of dreams. Dreams are real. They present us with an opportunity to try new things and see the world in new ways. When you look into dreams, you see how many choices are possible."

"Do my choices affect everything around me?" Karen asked.

"They certainly do. Each thread on this web connects to several others. You share your dreams with those closest to you, and can move in perfect harmony with those who are best connected to you. What you see here is the world as it really is, being created by all those who dream into reality their deepest fears and most secret desires."

"I saw myself at home in a possible reality where I didn't go to swim camp... what does that mean?" Karen asked.

"It means you wonder what might have been if you stayed home. What did you notice that was different?"

"I'd be reading lots of books, and feeling lonely."

"Every time you face big decisions in your life, you select a thread to follow, which leads you to interact with those who can help you most. Trust your intuition and your gut feelings, and they will lead you well."

Karen dreamt the rest of the night about the web of dreams, flying from one person's thoughts and feelings to another's. She watched these movies of the future play out every variation, and enjoyed noticing when paths were chosen and choices made. One loop of possibilities would end at that moment, and action would continue smoothly for a short time until the next decision point arrived. When Karen flew high above the web, she saw patterns as one person's choice affected every other part of the web of dreams.

Karen awoke very early the following morning to the sound of Gumdrop running on his wheel. She got up and dressed quickly, then went over and gave Wanda a shake, putting her finger to her lips and raising her eyebrows to indicate silence. When Wanda was dressed, they ran like the wind to see Gill and Charlotte.

Before they reached the cabin, Karen stopped in front of Wanda and said, "We'd better not mention visiting the cave to anyone. I'm pretty certain Gill and Charlotte had nothing to do with the explosives, but I feel better asking questions and gathering clues until I know for sure what's going on."

"OK, I'll let you do all the talking," Wanda agreed.

They arrived before the Shortgrasses began cooking breakfast, and Wanda listened as Karen breathlessly described her conversation with the voice in the lake.

Gill and Charlotte seemed interested yet relaxed, as if they were observing something they'd been expecting all along but enjoyed hearing nonetheless.

"So what should I do?" Karen asked.

"What feels right to you?" Gill countered.

"Well, I would feel better if I knew who was asking for help and what they needed. When I get answers to those questions I might have some idea of what I can do. Maybe the groundskeeper, Digger Drummond, can tell me more about what's down there."

"That's a good place to start," agreed Gill. "He lives in the woods on the other side of the camper's cabins. His place is small, like this one, and this is a good time to talk to him before he goes about his daily rounds."

"Thank you!" Karen said, giving Gill and Charlotte each a hug. She then turned and headed out the door with one last glance back to see the Shortgrasses wave to them through the window. Then she and Wanda ran back along the path to the opposite side of camp. The woods were different there. They seemed thicker and darker. She slowed her pace to a walk, so she could listen to every sound. She didn't hear any birds singing the way they did around the Shortgrass' cabin.

"Gill and Charlotte didn't put explosives in that cave," whispered Karen.

"How do you know?"

"They are peaceful people. And did you see how calm they were through our whole conversation? If they had something to hide, I would have felt their uneasiness." The girls walked together for a while in thoughtful silence.

I'm so glad you're coming with me," Karen said to Wanda as they approached Mr. Drummond's cabin.

"Are you kidding? I wouldn't miss this for the world!" Wanda murmured.

Karen grinned and replied, "I'm glad I don't have to pay you a million dollars!"

The lace curtains in the groundskeeper's cabin were drawn shut, and no smoke rose from the fireplace. "If I didn't know better, I'd think this cabin was unoccupied," said Karen.

"Look!" whispered Wanda, "There's something moving inside!" Both girls froze as a shadowy figure moved past the curtains in the front window. Working up all her courage, Karen stepped up to the door and knocked three times. There was a long silence before footsteps could be heard approaching, and the door swung slowly open.

"May I help you?" asked a tall, middle-aged man with a bald spot on the top of his head. He wore a dingy pair of coveralls over a clean yet grubby-looking long-sleeved work shirt. His voice crackled in a lilting singsong rhythm that rose and fell in a way that evoked an image of the hills and valleys of Scotland.

"Yes, I hope so!" replied, Karen. "Last night I heard a very strange sound coming from the lake. One of the swim campers told me that you might know something about it."

"Ahh, the wailing sound that comes at night!" Digger said, opening the door further and beckoning the girls to enter his cabin. "I know all about that, lassie. Come in and sit a spell, and I'll tell you what I've heard."

Karen and Wanda entered cautiously and sat down at the kitchen table. Mr. Drummond leaned back on the counter and gave them a lop-sided grin. "It's been a long time since I've spoken to anyone about it, but there is definitely something strange going on by that lake. Evil, some say it is, although there's been no proof of that. On the other hand, why would anyone want to find out? Ha!" Mr. Drummond's eyes gleamed as he spoke, and he stomped one foot emphasize his point.

Karen felt slightly ill, but tried to steady her

voice as she asked, "Have you just heard stories about this sound, or have you heard it yourself?"

"Yes, I've heard it, lassie, on numerous occasions, and always at night."

"And what has it said to you? Has it told you who it is or what it needs?"

"Now that is a tough one. I downa think anybody else heard it spak but mysell, although I've heard it many times." Digger paused to run his callused fingers through what thin hair he had left. "The first time I heard it, I was spooked half out of me wits. I jumped up and ran all the way back here, and didn't come out again 'til morning! The legend of this loch is that a long, long time ago, there was an evil spirit who challenged a sorcerer. The sorcerer was an Indian shaman, who was ill-sorted and turned out to have more skeel at working magic spells. The spell he cast sent the evil spirit straight down to the bottom of the loch, where it's been caught in its own trap ever since. Noo that's the story told to me by the last groundskeeper, and I wouldn'a believed naethin of it if I hadn't heard the scraugh with me own ears! It's a terrible sound, but I canna say that anythin' it says makes a bittock of sense."

Karen jumped at the sudden whistle of a black kettle on the stove.

"Where are me manners! Would you lassies like some tea or cocoa?" Digger asked as he went to the cupboard for mugs.

"Hot chocolate, thank you," Karen replied, as Wanda leaned across the table to hiss, "What about breakfast in the mess hall? We can't stay here too long, or we'll get in trouble!"

Karen put her finger to her lips and pleaded

with her eyes for Wanda to remain quiet just a while longer. Wanda sighed heavily, but said no more as Karen asked Digger, "If you were to guess what it was saying, what do you think it might be?"

"I downa ken. I canna imagine anything good coming from it, though. That skirling is most likely some kind of warning. I expect somegate it will rampage and attack someone, so if yeh care about yer life and limb, downa go to the loch at night. That's when its power is strongest."

Digger set two mugs of steaming hot cocoa down on the table and added, "And, lassie, I'd definitely run straight home if I ever heard it begin to skirl its awful song. Just listening to it could warp yer mind – and yeh might end up like the poor hapless travelers who heard the kelpies sing and their sense of direction went hirdie girdie before they stumbled into the loch and drowned."

Karen pondered what he said as she drank her cocoa, then suddenly exclaimed, "Goodness! It's breakfast time in the mess hall! ChaCha will be starting a search party for us if we don't get over there right now. Thanks so much for everything!"

"Now you remember what I told you, lassies. You may not get a second chance!" Digger called out to the girls as his front screen door banged shut behind them.

"Have you EVER heard anything like it?" giggled Karen. That grown man is scared of what's at the bottom of the lake!"

"I would be too, if I heard it wailing at me!" Wanda whimpered. "I think he's smart to stay away from the lake at night. You never know what might happen."

Web of Dreams

As the busy days of swim camp became more physically demanding, Karen swam so vigorously that she was exhausted at the end of each day. Every muscle ached when she awakened in the morning, and she kept sleeping in too late to visit Gill and Charlotte in the mornings. More than a week had passed since Karen and Wanda had visited Digger Drummond, and she felt a burning need to seek their advice for solving the mysteries of the lake. Karen was thrilled one morning to discover she'd awakened before the others, and crept quietly to Wanda's bunk to gently shake her awake.

"Let's go and see Gill and Charlotte," she whispered. Wanda nodded, rubbed her eyes, and quickly dressed. They ran together through the woods to the mess hall, leaping cross the golden sunbeams between the trees. When they got there, Gill and Charlotte were preparing breakfast.

Karen relayed what she'd heard from Digger Drummond and her voice had a disappointed edge as she concluded, "So I didn't learn anything useful."

Charlotte looked up in surprise and wiped her hands on her apron. "Really? You didn't see or hear *anything* to help you better understand what's going on?"

Karen could tell by the way Charlotte asked this question that she'd overlooked something, so she paused to review that morning's events. "Well, I learned that Digger is afraid of the voice that sings at night, because he feels he'll lose his mind if he listens to it, or that it might attack him."

"He thinks the wailing is a warning cry," Wanda added.

Charlotte brightened and Karen knew they were on the right track. "I learned that Digger cares about Wanda and I enough to warn us about something he feels might be very dangerous. When he talked about it, I felt ill. He lives so quietly in his cabin that it's hard to tell anyone is living there at all."

"You see? You learned many things from Mr. Drummond!"

"Yes, but I haven't made any progress in understanding the thing at the bottom of the lake. Worst of all, I don't know what to do next. I could go back again tonight, but it doesn't seem to want to answer my questions, and there's nobody else I can ask."

Gill set down his knife and looked straight at Karen. His voice was so smooth that it was almost hypnotic. "There is always someone you can ask. Go to the end of time. The Nothingness. The source of all that is and the balance point between all probabilities. There you will find that which you seek. Accept it. It is yours."

A long silence followed. Wanda looked at Gill as if he had two heads, and Karen tried to absorb this advice. She loved Gill, but sometimes he said really strange things that didn't make much sense. What could he mean by the end of time? She imagined a place where everything sprang forth into being. She guessed he didn't mean an actual place, but one she could go to in her mind. Perhaps this was the way to find out what she needed to know, and maybe she could dream herself to a place where the answer already existed.

Suddenly, Karen remembered her dream about the spider web. "I don't know what the end of time looks like, but I did have a dream about a spider web sparkling with dew where each drop contained a person and all the possibilities in their life."

"You've seen the dream weaver's web!" Gill exclaimed. "Yes, that is similar to what I mean about the end of time. There is a place we can go in which all possibilities exist simultaneously. We choose how our life unfolds after viewing many possibilities, and all these choices taken together create reality. You are very fortunate to have seen the dream weaver's web, for that is something few people even know exists. Once you know your place in the web of dreams, your life can become a dream come true. You can then awaken within your dreams."

Karen and Wanda sat silently, listening to Charlotte's pancakes sizzling on the grill.

"So when you say, 'Go to the end of time,' you mean we can be aware of much more than what's right in front of us?" Karen asked.

"Yes. It takes practice and conditioning of your mind. It helps a great deal to meditate. Have you ever meditated?"

"No," both girls replied simultaneously. Wanda asked, "What is 'meditate'?"

Charlotte replied, "Meditation is an exercise for calming the mind. You can start by observing each breath, and learning to sweep away all extraneous thoughts. Now is a perfect time to meditate! It's not as hard as it seems. One of my favorite places to meditate is out by the lake as the sun comes up. Find a comfortable place to sit, and pay attention to your breathing. Let go of any other thoughts that come along and try to distract you."

"You mean... this morning?" Wanda stammered.

"Why not? It's beautiful outside. I love to meditate surrounded by natural beauty. Now is the perfect time, while it's still quiet."

The girls exchanged glances, and Karen said, "Sounds great! Let's try it. Come on, Wanda!" They waved good-bye to Gill and Charlotte and walked together to a clearing in the forest by the lake. They sat down together on the soft grass. Karen tried to pay attention to her breathing, but every time she looked over at Wanda they'd both start to giggle.

"I don't think I'm doing this right," Wanda laughed.

"Every time I think of breathing and then look over at you I catch the giggles!" Karen agreed. "I bet this takes a lot of practice before we can get it right."

"WHY are we doing this, again?" Wanda asked.

"I think it's supposed to help us solve the mysteries of the lake. We need to calm our minds, and that's what meditation is supposed to help with."

"My mind needs a lot of calming!" Wanda

giggled as she rolled over onto her back and looked up at the blue sky.

"Every time I try to clear my thoughts, I keep seeing that cave. I'm starting to think we should tell someone about it."

"Me too," sighed Karen. "We could leave an anonymous note for ChaCha, warning her that the cave on the other side of the lake is full of explosives. She'll either go to investigate or not, but either way we'll know we've tried to tell her."

"But how will we find out who put it there? And what if she doesn't believe the note? Or worse yet, what if *she* is the one who put the explosives there? Unless we know who put those boxes there and why, they could easily do something even worse."

Karen sighed in exasperation, "Whoever put those explosives in the cave probably has a plan. They either want to wreck the lake and the swim camp, or perhaps they intend to blast the mountain looking for gold. Anyone who mines for gold or carries a grudge is a prime suspect."

Just then, three sharp blasts of a whistle sounded from the direction of the mess hall. "Maybe we'll get lucky and find another clue," said Karen, as she and Wanda walked back together to the mess hall. "Keep your eyes open for any suspicious activity – anything unusual or out of the ordinary."

When they reached the mess hall, they were greeted by Kirk and his gang of Flying Fish blocking the doorway. "Well if it isn't the smelliest Turd-el herself, with her little Turd-el Turd friend. Someone really should flush before the stink overwhelms us."

Wanda turned red with fury and looked for a moment like she wanted to do or say something horrible to Kirk. Karen's face flushed as well, but before either girl had a chance to utter a word, Julie emerged from the mess hall and said, "Just ignore those fried fish – there's a much better breakfast in here!"

Karen's eyes flashed at Kirk as she walked past, and he kicked his foot suddenly forward in an attempt to trip her, but she leaped neatly over his leg and curtsied. "It's such a pleasure dancing with you," she said in her most ladylike tone as his Flying Fish buddies hooted and laughed.

"I don't like them!" said Wanda, running to keep up behind Karen's long strides toward Julie, who was waiting in line at the food counter. "I wish there was something we could do to make them stop bothering us."

"Well you know what I always say," replied Julie. "If you can't beat 'em, join 'em!"

"What do you mean?" squealed Wanda, "You mean we should all turn into jerks too?"

"I simply mean we take the offensive! I have a few tricks up my sleeve!" replied Julie, as she accepted a plate of fresh strawberries and waffles from Charlotte.

Karen raised her eyebrows as she met Charlotte's gaze, hoping to silently convey her unspoken question, "What am I going to do about this?"

Charlotte laughed, as if she'd heard what was on Karen's mind, and found the situation funny. The older woman lowered her head slightly, and her eyes met Karen's. For a fraction of a second, Karen felt certain of Charlotte's response. It felt like she'd said, "You don't need to involve yourself in this. Just watch and learn." Karen smiled back and followed Julie and Wanda to the Turtles table.

By the time Karen sat down, Julie was excitedly whispering to Wanda about her plans for Kirk and the Flying Fish. "OK girls, here's the plan. We'll put some hot Tabasco sauce on a stick of cardboard that's cut in the shape of a stick of gum, and sprinkle it with powdered sugar. When we wrap it up in a gum wrapper, Kirk will think it's a stick of gum, and when he puts it in his mouth, he'll need the fire department to save his tongue!"

Just then, Mike entered the mess hall looking thoroughly distracted. Karen followed his gaze across the room to Jasper, who was walking to the food counter for her breakfast plate. She noticed him staring at her, and tilted and lowered her head flirtatiously before turning her attention back to her food.

"He's in love!" gushed Julie. "I don't think he can even walk straight!" Sure enough, Mike tripped over the leg of the Water Snakes' bench. Jasper seemed oblivious to the commotion as Mike sheepishly picked himself up. She breezed by him and joined the River Otters table as Mike stooped down to retrieve something shiny and gold from the floor, and put it in his pocket.

Karen and Wanda exchanged meaningful glances, and Karen sidled up to Mike.

Mike regained a semblance of dignity and rose to strike a spoon on a water glass. "Attention everyone!" he called out. "You've all done a great job of improving your swim strokes, and every cabin still has an excellent chance at winning the Lovell Cup. I expect to see some Olympic quality swimming out there this afternoon, campers." At this, Mike turned his head toward Jasper, who was smiling back at him from the River Otters table, and flushed crimson. "That's all."

Karen looked up at Mike and asked, "Do you know if there's any gold in the hills around here?"

Mike looked momentarily disoriented by the question, and coughed before answering. "There might be some gold around here, but I don't think it's easy to get to. You'd pretty much have to sift through every stone in the hills, and it would hardly be worth the effort. Why do you ask?"

"My friend bet me that there isn't any, but I told her I was pretty sure there is." Karen replied. "I thought perhaps you'd found a nugget here at Lake Lovell."

"You mean THIS?" Mike asked, retrieving the piece of gold from his pocket. "This is a gold good luck charm given to me by my grandfather, and I never go anywhere without it. He was a gold prospector in California, and this was the biggest nugget he ever found panning for gold."

Karen shook her head, "No," as she walked back to Wanda and followed the other kids outdoors toward the lake.

The morning practice swim was refreshing for Karen, and she welcomed the opportunity to hone her skills and take her mind off the thing at the bottom of the lake. Wanda didn't seem to have Karen's confidence that whatever it is wouldn't attack them as they swam, even though Karen had reassured her several times.

At first, Wanda had not looked at all convinced, but gradually she'd forgotten to worry.

Karen was encouraged to find that she could master new swim strokes simply by telling herself she was already good at them. It became a game she played with Wanda. "I'm really good at the back stroke," Karen would say. "Yes you are," Wanda would reply. And, "I can do the butterfly perfectly."

"I'm great at the Australian crawl," Karen replied, continuing to be amazed at how well this technique worked, even when they both got the giggles at their outrageous assertions of swimming prowess. She made a mental note to try this out when she began fifth grade in the fall.

Lunchtime came quickly, and before they knew it, it was time for the afternoon races.

A Good Sport

Karen felt proficient enough at swimming after weeks of practice to watch the other teams during the daily races as they swam their relay laps, and what she saw one afternoon caused her to look twice. She moved closer to Julie and in a low voice said, "Look! The Flying Fish aren't tagging each other and passing the bracelet like they're supposed to." Julie frowned and turned to watch as Kirk swam from the raft back to shore. Sure enough, when he was within a few strokes of reaching land, the next boy on his team dove into the water without receiving the colored bracelet.

"They're CHEATING!" exclaimed Julie, "We've got to tell Sondra!"

Karen and Julie ran together to where Sondra stood. "Sondra," Karen said in a low voice, "When you get a chance, take a look at the Flying Fish. They're not passing their bracelet."

"In two words, THEY CHEAT!" shouted Julie, shaking with vehemence.

Sondra looked over just in time to see the next boy in line dive into the water without putting on the blue bracelet. She shook her head, and walked over to Steve, who was squinting through his designer sunglasses.

"Steve, you need to check out your swimmers," she began, but Steve hushed her and continued gazing out into the middle of the lake. She turned to see what he was staring at, but there didn't seem to be anything there.

"They're jumping over there. I just saw a big one!" he said in his low voice.

"Who are jumping?" Sondra asked.

"Trout. Big ones. I wish I could take my pole over there and catch some for dinner tonight!" Steve brushed a stray lock of his blonde hair back into place.

Sondra gazed out across the lake, and still didn't see anything jumping.

"Steve, forget the fish! I've seen several of your guys taking off without their bracelets, and you know what that means."

Steve looked at his swim team and immediately saw what was going on. He blew his whistle and shouted, "The jig's up, guys! Everyone out of the water!" At this loud announcement, people from the other teams stared at the Flying Fish. Shouts of "No fair!" and "Cheaters!" filled the air. They were silenced by a blast from ChaCha's golden whistle signaling the end of the race. The expression on her face was stern as she announced the winners. "The Flying Fish finished first, but will be disqualified due to their failure to pass the bracelet. The Turtles came in second, so they are the winners for the day. Water Snakes win second place, and River Otters take third. I am very proud of all of you who swam according to the rules of the race, and extremely disappointed in those of you who felt a need to cheat. I expect much better from you tomorrow. I expect you to be good sports and swim to the best of your ability."

Karen saw Andy walking with his head hung low. "What happened out there?" she asked him. She could hardly believe that Andy would cheat. His voice trembled. "Kirk and his friends took our bracelet and wouldn't pass it on, so the only way we could race was to just pretend we had it. I didn't know what to do, so I just took my turn like the others at about the right time." Andy implored, "Please believe me – I wasn't trying to cheat!"

"You did everything you could. I'd probably have done the same thing, " Karen offered sympathetically, shuddering at the thought.

"Hey, Karen! Are you coming?" Julie called.

"I'll see you later!" Karen waved to Andy. She wrapped herself in her towel and ran to catch up with Julie, Wanda, and Gina. "Those Flying Fish are out of the frying pan and into the fire," laughed Julie. "But if Kirk thinks this is hot, wait 'til he sinks his teeth into my special Tabasco gum!"

Gina and Julie exchanged knowing glances, and Gina added gleefully, "He won't suspect anything until it's too late!"

Karen showered and changed, then left her teammates to their chewing gum project. As she walked out the door of the Turtles cabin, Wanda called after her. "Hey! Wait for me! Can I come too?"

"If you're ready right now!" Karen replied and paused on the cabin porch to hold the door.

They arrived at the mess hall as long shadows stretched across the trails and the sky turned brilliant shades of pink and orange. Gill and Charlotte greeted the girls with hugs, and Charlotte asked, "So how is your meditation coming along?"

Both girls broke into gales of giggles at this question, and Karen gasped, "We couldn't stop laughing!"

Charlotte smiled and continued rinsing off some vegetables in the sink. "The important thing is that you tried it out. Paying attention only to your breathing can be difficult at first for anyone – that's why practice makes such a difference. When I first tried to meditate, I kept thinking of important things I thought I needed to be doing, so I'd only meditate for a few minutes at a time. It took me years to meditate for up to an hour." Charlotte carried the rinsed vegetables to Gill, who was chopping them into bite-sized pieces.

"Does it ever get any easier?" Karen asked, "Meditation, I mean."

Gill laughed a surprisingly deep belly laugh, and replied, "The more I know about it, the more I realize how much I don't know!" His eyes sparkled, and for the first time Karen felt she really knew what he meant.

Before Karen could say anything in reply, Julie and Gina arrived at the kitchen door, breathless from running. "Hello!" gasped Julie, her eyes shining with mischievous delight. "We'd like to borrow a few drops of Tabasco sauce and some powdered sugar if you could spare it, please."

Gill looked up from his chopping and asked, "Are you *sure* you want to take the next step in this dance?"

Julie's eyebrows shot up at the question, "What?!"

"You don't have to dance with anybody who

114

asks." He smiled.

Julie looked even more baffled, but shrugged as Charlotte returned to the door with the bottle of hot sauce and a baggie with some powdered sugar in it. "He means you might want to think twice about what you're planning to do," she said in a soft voice.

Julie's eyes regained their usual look of confidence and she flashed her most dazzling smile. "Oh, we're sure, all right! We're totally and completely 100% sure! Thank you SO much for these! We'll get the hot sauce back to you right away!" She waved at Charlotte before turning to run down the path back to the Turtle's cabin.

With a hasty "Thank you!" Gina turned and ran giggling after Julie.

Karen spun around to face Gill. "How do you know what they're up to?"

With his eyes shut, Gill replied, "I see pictures in their minds of how they wish to provoke a boy with mischief."

Karen's eyes widened in wonder that Gill could see so clearly. "Wow, what else do you see?"

"I see you are worried about something you haven't told me about," he replied.

Karen flushed crimson red, and looked down at her toes. "Yes, I have been worried about something, but I didn't know how to tell you about it." Karen sighed and continued, "I was afraid I'd get in trouble, so I thought it would be best not to mention it."

"I see an image in your mind of a dark place full of danger."

Karen blushed even more, and looked up to

meet Gill's eyes. "Yes, I swam across the lake and followed the writing on the rock to a cave entrance. I went up some stone steps, and saw thirty boxes of explosives stored inside the cave. Only Wanda and I know about this, because I've been too afraid to tell anyone... I didn't know who I could trust."

"You can trust us," Charlotte said, walking over to give Karen a hug.

The moment Charlotte hugged Karen, Karen felt as if a tremendous weight had been lifted. She was surprised to feel how wet her eyes had become, and how glad she was to be free of the burden of carrying the secret of the cave.

"There is a way you can see with your mind, and not just your eyes, if you are ready," Gill stated quietly.

Karen felt unable to speak, and silently nodded her assent.

"Sit down and close your eyes," Gill continued.

Karen felt goose bumps run up and down her arms. She sat down and closed her eyes, allowing herself to become accustomed to the darkness. She heard Wanda pull a chair over alongside her.

Karen softly murmured, "I still can't believe I saw that writing on the boulder by the lake in my dreams, and then it turned out to be real."

"When you stop doubting your senses, you will become more sure of yourself," Gill replied. "Breathe out your doubt and breathe in a sense of who you truly are – the spirit that lives forever and now shines through you. Spirit sees through all things. Spirit sees without eyes and hears without ears. There are no secrets to Spirit.

116

When you wish to see clearly and know truth, you can see what you most need to know."

Karen did as he suggested. When she exhaled, she imagined she was breathing out her fear of the hooded man, her worry about the cave full of explosives, her resentment of how things were at home, her irritation at the Flying Fish for cheating, and her concern about what she could do to help the thing at the bottom of the lake. She breathed in, imagining she could see farther than just this room. She imagined that she was the living embodiment of Spirit, capable of seeing without using her eyes and hearing without using her ears. She waited for the magical result, but there was none. "I don't see anything different," she finally muttered after several minutes had elapsed and she had seen nothing other than darkness. She rubbed her eyes briefly and added, "Maybe I'm not doing it right."

"I don't see anything either," whined Wanda. "Just the dark red insides of my eyes with little flashes of light every now and then."

"You see more when you relax. Give it a bit more time," Charlotte intoned with a musical lilt to her voice. "You will adjust to the silence within all things and soon have the answers you seek. Follow the love you feel... those lines of love connect each of us to one another."

Karen squeezed her eyes shut more tightly, as if that would help her see beyond this room.

"Don't try too hard," said Charlotte. "Just relax."

Karen exhaled deeply and did as Charlotte recommended. For several minutes, she didn't notice anything different. The most difficult thing was keeping her mind focused as it constantly attempted to wander off. She found herself wondering what Gumdrop was doing and whether Julie and Gina got all the ingredients they needed for their secret project. She heard her stomach growl and wondered if it would be OK if she asked for a before-dinner snack. She exhaled again. "I keep thinking of all sorts of other things besides what I want to see," she complained.

"That is just the normal flow of the mind," Charlotte told her. "When a thought arises, just let it go. Don't worry. Anything important will come back to you later. Recognize each distracting thought and let it drift away again, so you can return your attention to what you most need to know."

Karen noticed herself wondering whether she'd put on a clean T-shirt or one she'd already worn. This time, instead of allowing it to bother her, she let that thought drift on through. She wasn't going to think about anything right now, except what she most needed to know – who or what was trapped at the bottom of Lovell Lake? Karen thought to herself, *there is a connection of love between me and whoever that is, so all I need to do is follow it.*

It seemed to be working! Karen heard the roaring and felt the familiar tingling sensation moving up and down her body. She pushed her right foot gently down into the floor and felt it sinking through the floorboards. She wiggled her toes, and felt the long nails holding the boards down. She noticed how good it felt to be barefoot and pulled her foot back out of the floor. The roaring noise and waves of vibration gradually diminished, but she felt fully relaxed, energized, and ready to get to the bottom of the mystery in the lake.

With a sharp "Click!" Karen floated up out of her body and took a moment to observe the scene in the mess hall kitchen. Gill looked up directly at her and smiled, so Karen smiled back and winked. She was amazed to see Gill return the wink. Her body remained seated in the chair next to Wanda, but she was no longer aware of its physical sensations. She took one last look at the room, noticing Wanda fidgeting with her hair and shuffling her feet. Then, with a deep breath, Karen's dream body moved up through the ceiling of the mess hall kitchen and out over the lake, right near the spot where the sounds had seemed to originate. She felt the cold night breeze on her skin, and the cloth of her T-shirt and jeans flapping as she hovered over the water. She listened deeply, and again, she heard it. "Help me! Please help me!"

Karen reminded herself that things weren't normal. It was like she was in a dream, but she hadn't been to sleep. This was the most real-to-life daydream she'd ever had, because her senses felt much sharper than usual. The lake sparkled with a dozen shades of blue. There was a vibrant energy surrounding every rock, tree and flower that looked like colorful rainbows of fire. And the sounds! Even though she was in the middle of the lake, she could hear its soothing lap against the shore underlying the rustling wind and the song of frogs, bats, and crickets. Nature seemed to be playing a symphony just for her. She'd never realized that the lake had a scent, but it did, although just what it smelled like, she couldn't say. She could feel every cell in her body, could hear her soft heart beat and the rhythmic swooshes of her blood through her veins and her breath through her lungs. It was amazing! She took one more deep breath, and then dove down into the silvery waters of Lovell Lake.

Roggum

Karen was acutely aware of how the water felt against her feet as she half-swam, half-flew downwards to the bottom of Lake Lovell, and was glad to be barefoot. She had to keep reminding herself that this was "just a dream," that, really, she was in the mess hall kitchen with Gill and Charlotte standing next to her and Wanda sitting there at the table. When she looked around, though, what she saw was not familiar faces but bits of algae, twigs and leaves floating by in the water, as well as an occasional school of fish. The fish didn't seem to mind her being there and ignored her as she continued her descent.

Down, down, down Karen went, and still there was farther to go. This lake was much deeper than she had imagined. It was almost as if it had no bottom at all. For a brief moment, Karen panicked. Was she plummeting to her doom? She reassured herself that Gill and Charlotte would not encourage her to do anything truly dangerous, and the thought mustered her courage.

As she continued her descent, Karen saw a glowing yellow light below her. She felt butterflies in her stomach and slowed down. Tall fronds of sea grass were growing at the bottom of the lake, and there amidst the watery foliage was a large glowing orb, with someone – or something – trapped inside!

"You've come! My hero! I am saved!" cried a furry human-shaped creature crouching inside the glowing ball. Karen was about to reply, when she realized she would not be able to speak properly under water. With her mind she sent the thought, "Who are you? How did you get here?"

The furry one replied, "My name is Roggum. I am an ancient spirit who exists only to help men, yet one of those I served treated me cruelly and imprisoned me here at the bottom of this lake."

"But if you are spirit, why can't you just free yourself?" thought Karen in response.

"Alas, I have not the strength. If there was the support of those who knew and loved me, I would have been able to escape centuries ago, but they are all long dead, and uncaring about the fate of poor Roggum." Roggum's baleful eyes gazed up at Karen with an expression of deep sorrow.

"But some people *can* hear you! Digger Drummond, the groundskeeper, is so scared by your wailing at night that he only comes out in the day!"

"Woe! Woe is me!" exclaimed Roggum, flailing about inside the glowing orb. "I am strong enough to be heard by some in my time of deepest despair, and all they do is hide!"

"Well, your cries are very scary," Karen explained gently with her mind. "What's worse is the rumor that you once challenged an Indian shaman who figured out what you were doing and caught you in your own trap!" She felt her

122

face flush hot as she wondered if she'd be able to tell if Roggum lied to her. She hoped she hadn't said too much.

Roggum slouched into a rumpled pile of fur at the bottom of the orb. He was perfectly silent and reminded Karen of the limp remains of a balloon whose air had been released. She felt sorry for him, even though she suspected that might be a mistake. If it were true that Roggum had once tried to trick a shaman, what would prevent him from trying to trick her? In spite of these questions, she moved closer and pressed her hands up against the orb's smooth, glowing walls. It felt blubbery, like she imagined the skin of a dolphin or whale would feel. As she ran her hands across its surface, the areas she touched darkened, and she could see her handprints spreading out on the surface of the ball.

"Don't do that! Don't touch the orb!" squealed Roggum.

Karen was surprised by his sudden outburst, and withdrew her hands. "Why not?" she asked.

"You'll drain the energy, and I might die in here!" Roggum squawked. He suddenly became much more animated, which Karen felt was a good thing. It seemed more likely that he would answer her questions now.

"Is it true that you tried to trick someone to come down here to the bottom of this lake and be trapped here, but you got trapped instead?" she demanded.

Roggum hid his face behind his large furry hands. He moaned loudly, but didn't say anything Karen could understand.

"If you don't answer me, I'll have to touch the orb again."

"Not that! Anything but that!" pleaded Roggum, once again hopping about in a lively fashion. "OK, OK, I'll tell you. It's true. I didn't want to tell you because I was afraid if you knew the truth, then you wouldn't help me, but you already know. Woe is me! Woe is me!"

"Now, now," Karen soothed. "It's better to tell the truth and let people decide for themselves what to do." Then with growing confidence she added, "If you expect someone to love you enough to free you, you'll need to be honest with them."

Roggum sighed and sank back down to the bottom of his orb. "So does this mean you will help me?" he asked, looking up at her, "I'd like to help you," Karen replied. A huge commotion erupted inside the orb. Roggum leaped and bounded about so frenetically that the blubber walls shook like Jell-o. The walls oscillated wildly with his frenzied dance of ecstasy and Karen's smile turned into a laugh. She swallowed a bit of water and was suddenly aware of a strong need to return to her body in the mess hall kitchen. As soon as the thought came, she found herself flying back up out of the lake, emerging from the water with a leaping arc, the way she'd seen trout in the lake jump. She hovered over the lake for several seconds before flying back to the mess hall and down through the ceiling into her body, which she entered with a sucking sensation.

A few moments later, Karen felt a tingling surge of energy beginning in her toes and legs, then rising up to her chest, arms, and head. The tingling united Karen's flying self with her body, and she suddenly remembered two sets of memories from the last twenty minutes. She recalled hearing Wanda shuffling her feet and sniffling as Gill and Charlotte moved around in the kitchen preparing the evening meal, and she also remembered every bit of her conversation with Roggum at the bottom of Lake Lovell.

Karen opened her eyes, and saw Gill and Charlotte's faces beaming back at her. "You did it!" Gill said softly, his eyes shining with pride.

Karen was so excited to tell the Shortgrasses what had transpired that she bounced around like Roggum, waving her arms as she described the size, shape, and texture of the orb. She re-enacted Roggum's movements to show his personality, and Gill and Charlotte watched and listened intently with laughing eyes. Karen couldn't get over the sense that they already knew what had taken place.

Wanda's eyes were huge with wonder as she listened to Karen's story, yet when it was done, the corners of her mouth drooped downwards and she bit her lower lip. "All I saw was the inside of my eyelids, and all I heard was the sound of dinner cooking in the kitchen," she moaned.

"That's a good place to start," reassured Charlotte, as she patted Wanda on the head. "IF you really want to, you can travel anywhere."

Karen's eyes were shining as she turned to Gill. "I winked at you when I was floating up by the ceiling in this room, and I saw you look straight at me and wink back. Could you see me while I was flying around? What did I look like to you?"

Gill grinned more broadly than Karen had ever seen him smile before. "Yes, child, I could see you! You looked pale, like a ghost made of fog, but your face shone like the moon! If you had spoken to me, I would have heard every word you said."

"Wow," exclaimed Wanda, looking back and forth between Gill and Karen in obvious amazement.

Their discussion was interrupted by the sounds of people entering the mess hall, so Karen gave Gill and Charlotte big hugs, and she and Wanda joined the Turtles in line for dinner.

"Did that all seem just as real to you as this?" Wanda whispered to Karen as the girls reached for their trays.

"Sort of." replied Karen. "In some ways, I felt like I was dreaming while awake, so everything was just like in a dream, but it was even a bit more real, if you know what I mean. In another way, I'm not sure I wasn't just imagining the whole thing."

"I wish I could do that," sighed Wanda. "I know I have a good imagination, but I couldn't imagine anything besides how good dinner is going to taste tonight."

"If Charlotte says you can learn, then I'm sure it's true."
"How did you get to be so good at it so fast?"

I've been good at dreaming for as long as I can remember," Karen told her, "but I don't really know what I'm doing. Gill and Charlotte are helping me trust my senses – and believe what I experience is real."

The girls stopped talking as Julie and Gina joined them. Karen noticed with amusement that they were tracking Kirk's every motion as he moved through the mess hall. They were like a couple of cats watching a bird hopping through the grass, thought Karen, while Kirk was oblivious. He came in at the center of a group of his buddies, and did a little dance on top of one of the dining table benches, and then joined the end of the dinner line.

"Act normal!" Julie whispered to Gina and Wanda, as they looked away from Kirk and doubled over with giggles.

"That IS fairly normal for them," Karen laughed, as she took a plate of lasagna, salad, and vegetables from Charlotte.

Dinner seemed to take longer than usual, as Julie waited with tense anticipation for the right moment to ask Kirk if he'd like a stick of gum. People began putting their plates and trays up on the end of the counter in the mess hall, when Julie hissed, "Now!" and rose from the Turtle's table. She strode purposefully over to where Kirk was stretching after finishing his meal, and said, "Hi there! Would you like a stick of gum?"

Julie took one stick out of the pack, and casually popped it into her mouth. She offered the pack to Kirk, with one stick extended a bit beyond the others.

"Sure... why not?" mumbled Kirk, as he reached for the gum. Slowly, he unwrapped it. Julie held her breath as he stood for several long moments and studied it before popping it into his mouth. Within two seconds, the expression on his face changed. His chewing seemed labored and his eyes began to water. He looked confused and then furious as he spat the gum out onto the floor.

Julie and Gina and Wanda doubled over laughing, as Kirk coughed and gasped, "Water!"

One of the boys from the Flying Fish table passed him a glass, which he drank straight down in seven gulps. Karen started to say something, but she could tell from the look on Kirk's face that it would only make things worse, so she just stood silently as the other Turtles laughed and left the mess hall. She was still standing there when Wanda grabbed her by the sleeve whispering, "Come ON!" and pulled her out through the mess hall doors.

Back at the Turtles cabin, Julie was triumphant. "Whoo-hoo!" she shouted as she recounted the story of her chewing gum trick over and over. The other Turtles whooped and laughed along with her, until Sondra entered the room.

"Lights out, girls," she said firmly, and stood with her hand on the switch until all the Turtles were in their bunks.

Karen shut her eyes and felt herself beginning to drift off. She thought she heard someone calling her name over and over again and knew the muffled cry came from beneath the lake.

Awakening

On Thursday morning, Karen awoke in a tangle of sheets with fragmented memories of several fitful dreams. The details were lost, and all she could recollect was that they involved Kirk, Roggum, the explosives, and Ohgeenay, and she felt disappointed. She was sweating, and judging from the mess she'd made of her bed covers, she'd been tossing and turning for hours. She couldn't shake the feeling that something was dreadfully wrong, although she didn't know what it was or how to fix it. The end of swim camp was fast approaching, and Karen could hardly believe how time had flown by.

Karen was thrilled to find she was the first one in the Turtle cabin to wake up. She looked over at Gumdrop's cage and was relieved to see he was curled in a comfortable ball with his head tucked down alongside his tail. After watching his furry back rise and fall ever so slightly with each breath, she unlatched the cage door and reached over to stroke him. He jumped, startled at her unexpected touch, and looked up to see her smiling down at him. He stretched and yawned luxuriously, then licked the fur on his left flank. Karen quietly latched the cage and blew a silent kiss to him.

Karen dressed quickly and ran down the trail to see Gill and Charlotte. She felt desperate to talk with them, because she sensed they could help her sort out the confusion she was feeling. She knocked softly on their cabin door, and when there was no answer, poked her head inside. "Gill? Charlotte?" The cabin was empty.

Karen's heart was already pounding from having run the whole distance from her cabin to theirs, and now it felt like it was trying to jump right out of her chest. She checked the bedroom and looked in their bathroom, but no one was there. She hadn't seen them as she ran past the mess hall, which looked dark and empty. *Where could they be?*

Karen sat down at the kitchen table and cradled her head in her hands. She needed to calm herself and think clearly. *Had something happened to them? Was this the reason her dreams had been so upsetting? Had Roggum gotten loose and trapped them at the bottom of the lake? Where could they have gone before breakfast?*

Karen's mind raced with questions. She really needed to talk to Gill and Charlotte and had no idea where they had gone. Tears welled up in her eyes. She felt so alone. The longer she sat there, the more upset she became. She visualized herself crying here in the kitchen until they returned just barely in time to prepare breakfast. She then imagined that they didn't come back, and saw herself walking back to her cabin to cry and being surrounded by well-intentioned Turtles who had no idea what she was feeling. She felt that no one but Gill and Charlotte knew her well enough to understand her feelings.

Weren't they always supposed to be here for her? She'd just assumed they would be. Didn't they know how much she was counting on talking to them this morning? They'd always seemed to know what she was feeling before. Karen's despair felt total as she lay her head down in her arms on their kitchen table.

After several minutes that seemed like an eternity of sorrow, Karen had the thought that this could be an opportunity to practice what she was learning. Maybe she could find out where they were by quieting her mind and focusing on feeling the bond of love between herself and them. Perhaps she could use the same technique she'd used to find the cave entrance and to see Roggum at the bottom of the lake, and could go to them.

She shut her eyes and felt her heart glowing with love for the Shortgrasses. She remembered how glad she felt when she saw them and the way it felt when they hugged her. She breathed out her fear and breathed in more and more love.

With her eyes still shut, she saw an image of wildflowers by the side of the lake. Charlotte and Gill were walking hand in hand along the water's edge. Karen's eyes popped open, and she bounded up with a laugh. Of course! They'd gone to gather some flowers for their table!

She ran outside and, after a moment's hesitation, down the trail that felt right. She couldn't see them, but followed her feet as they led her along the lakeside trail. She loped along at a steady pace, looking around for some sign of her friends.

Within a few minutes, she saw them walking toward her. She sped up, quickly closing the distance between them. "Hey!" she cried, happy to be reunited with them.

"Hello, hello!" called Charlotte, opening her arms to give the laughing girl a big welcoming hug.

"I didn't know where you were!" exclaimed Karen. "I had nightmares last night, and then when you weren't at the cabin I felt so afraid!"

"So how did you manage to find us?" asked Charlotte.

"Well, I did like you told me. I felt my love for you, closed my eyes, and tried to see where you were and what you were doing!"

Charlotte smiled and Gill said, "Now it's obvious that you're definitely not a sleepwalker!"

Karen blushed with pride.

"So, what did you dream?" asked Charlotte.

"I dreamed about the explosives... and Kirk, and Ohgeenay, and Roggum. They were all angry with me."

"It sounds like you remember the dream very well," said Charlotte.

"Not exactly," Karen admitted. I can't remember what happened. That's just a blur, but I woke up feeling like something is terribly wrong and I don't know how to fix it. I know Kirk is upset with me because he thinks I was in on the gum prank. Roggum is still waiting to be rescued from the bottom of the lake, and I have no idea how to do that or even if it's a good idea, and Ohgeenay is a spirit I don't trust at all. I still have no idea who put explosives in the cave."

When they reached the Shortgrass cabin, Gill held the heavy wooden door open for Charlotte and Karen to enter. "You are sensing the feelings of others who feel wronged by you," Gill told her quietly.

"Yes!" said Karen, sighing heavily and collapsing into one of the kitchen chairs.

"You feel how angry and disappointed they are with you, and you feel troubled by that," he continued.

"That's it exactly," Karen nodded, feeling much better that someone understood. Her sense of panic was dissipating now that Gill was stating her feelings so clearly.

"And you sense that if you do nothing, one or another of them will do something bad to you," he concluded.

"What can I do?" Karen implored in a howling wail. She hadn't meant to howl like that, but her feelings of panic were returning again.

"You can ask for help and protection from those who love you. All you ever need do is ask with all your heart, and help will be with you."

Hearing that made Karen feel a little better, although she still had a strong premonition of danger. "Is there any way to prevent them from causing trouble?" she asked Gill.

"Sometimes, things seem to go wrong, so that we can learn something we would never have experienced otherwise. We gain strength when we are challenged."

Gill put on his apron, and the three of them made their way toward the mess hall.

"I have a sinking feeling, like something awful is about to happen," Karen said.

"Your dream described ways you can resolve your differences, and how you will weave this web of your waking dream with others. Choices can feel difficult when you honor the feelings of those you have been avoiding. That could explain why you awakened feeling so upset this morning."

"You mean I agreed to something I don't want to do?" demanded Karen, feeling like her stomach was doing flip-flops.

"You have mixed feelings about it," agreed Gill with a nod of his head.

Karen softly moaned and rubbed her eyes, which still ached from crying. She stumbled right into Julie, who exclaimed, "Watch where you're going! You almost knocked this out of my hand!" as she gave the borrowed bottle of Tabasco sauce to Gill.

"What's the matter with you?" Julie asked. "You look like you've been bawling."

"Nothing's wrong," Karen muttered. "I just didn't sleep well last night."

"Wow, for a minute there, I thought you were walking to breakfast in your sleep!"

Karen smiled at this, and quickly searched Julie's face to see if there was any additional meaning in her words. There didn't appear to be, but she felt better to hear a reminder about sleepwalkers. After all, Gill had just told her this morning that she definitely wasn't one.

"Why don't you come with us, Karen? Gina and Wanda and I are going down to the pier before breakfast to see if we can spot the monster in the lake!"

Karen looked up sharply, wondering how Julie knew about the spirit at the bottom of the lake. She looked at Gill, but his tranquil face was unreadable. Karen was mildly annoyed with Wanda for having talked about the legend of Lake Lovell's trapped spirit with Julie. "OK," she said weakly, "but I don't think it's a monster." Then with a shrug at Gill and Charlotte, she followed Julie down the path to the lake.

"Wanda told us what Digger Drummond said," Julie boasted, "and I want to hear the beast roar for myself!"

Karen sighed, feeling that there was no easy way she could tell Julie about how she'd met Roggum in person. For that matter, she still had no idea what to do for him. In all the morning's excitement, she'd had no opportunity to ask Gill and Charlotte's advice.

"The wailing is only supposed to happen at night," Karen reminded her.

"That's what they say, but it makes no sense to me," Julie replied in a conspiratorial tone. "If something is really trapped down there, why wouldn't it call for help in the daytime, too?"

They were now close enough to the lake to see the early morning sunshine sparkling on its waves. Gina and Wanda were standing at the water's edge, and they waved as Julie and Karen approached.

"Hey, you guys!" Karen turned at the sound of Andy's familiar voice. She was delighted to see him approaching with his brother, Ben. "That was pretty cool what you did to Kirk with that stick of gum, Julie! That was the first time I've seen him at a loss for words!" Andy screwed up his face to imitate Kirk's expressions as he'd chewed the stick of cardboard, then pretended to spit it out in disgust as he fell to the ground clutching his throat with both hands and gasping hoarsely, "Water!"

Julie howled with laughter, and slapped her thighs as Karen and Ben just smiled.

Andy got up and dusted himself off before continuing, "Kirk was furious when he got back to the cabin. I heard him say something about getting even. If I were you, I'd watch my backside."

"Kirk's no problem for us," Julie replied. "He should know not to mess with Turtles!" Karen wished she felt as confident. In fact, at Andy's words, her stomach knotted, and she felt a premonition that something terrible was going to happen.

"Did he say anything about what he is planning to do?" she asked Andy.

"Nope. Just that somebody will pay for this. Knowing Kirk, he'll think up something pretty nasty that will make lots of people wish he'd stayed home this summer."

Just then, the familiar toot from ChaCha's whistle signaled that breakfast was being served, and the six friends walked together to the mess hall.

Makai-mo

Karen's feelings of alarm stayed with her all through the morning meal. Julie, on the other hand, reveled in Kirk's recent embarrassments. She was in such a jovial mood that she even whooped twice, causing Karen's stomach to lurch. Karen sensed that for some reason Kirk held her responsible for the gum incident. She felt caught between the desire to tell Kirk she had nothing to do with it and to stay quiet and loyal to Julie and the other Turtles. By the time the morning swimming lessons began, she felt so ill that she asked Sondra if she could sit on the beach for a while. The counselor looked concerned. "Do you feel sick? What hurts?"

"I didn't sleep very well, and my stomach hurts."

Sondra sat down on the sand next to Karen and rubbed her back for a few minutes. "You'll feel a lot better if you get some rest. Just watch the others, and imagine how each of the swim strokes feels. I'll come back and check on you in a while." Sondra handed Karen her towel and said, "Wrap yourself in this; it will keep you warm."

Karen sighed in relief at the chance to collect her thoughts. She closed her eyes and immediately sensed Roggum's presence. She saw him enclosed in his underwater bubble, and heard him say, "It's about time! I thought you'd forgotten all about me!"

Karen thought back in response, "I haven't forgotten you. I just don't know how to help. Can you tell me exactly how you got trapped in the first place? That might help me figure out how to free you."

Roggum sank down on his haunches. "Well, it all began when an Indian medicine man named Makai-mo kept calling me to help him. He had me running errand after errand until I felt like my feet were going to fall off. When he told me to gather armloads of grass from the bottom of this lake, I decided he'd gone too far. I was about to tell him he'd just have to do that little task himself. Then I thought about how nice it would be to be free of his demands once and for all, so I created this bubble and told him I needed his help. 'I don't know how to gather that lake grass,' I lied. 'Could you come down and help me with it?'

"At first he said, 'no,' but I insisted, so he finally agreed and accompanied me to the bottom of the lake on what I hoped would be his last trip. Unfortunately, he read my mind and knew about what I was up to, and before I could say skipdoodle-a-wingding, he'd put me in the very trap I had made for him. It all happened so fast that I can't tell you what he did, I just know my head was spinning for months afterwards, and then the months stretched into years, which stretched into decades. I don't even know how long I've been down here now, but I hope it's not too late to offer an apology."

"I don't know," said Karen, "Maybe it's not. I have friends who tell me that nobody ever really dies, and if that's true, we can call on Makai-mo to talk with us. Maybe we can convince him to release you."

Roggum moaned and wailed, and Karen thought, "Shhh! Don't make too much noise! Don't you want to be free again?"

"Yes!" wailed Roggum.

"I think this is the only way to get you out of there, so just wait a moment while I ask the medicine man's spirit to join us." She kept her eyes shut and felt her connection of love with the shaman. She visualized him from Roggum's story, softly said his name "Makai-mo" aloud four times, and waited. After several moments, she felt a breeze softly flap her towel.

"I am here," she heard a new voice say in her mind.

"Thank you for coming," Karen thought to Makai-mo. "I am hoping you will help free Roggum from this underwater trap. He wants to apologize to you for what he did many years ago."

In Karen's mind's eye, she saw a tall Indian brave standing alongside her on the beach. He looked strong and stern and wore an expression of impassive indifference.

"I put him there because he is dangerous to humans." Makai-mo replied. "He shall remain, until he learns to respect those he serves." Roggum whimpered, but said nothing.

"How can you tell when he is ready to respect people?" thought Karen.

"By the way he interacts with them," replied Makai-mo.

"But how can he freely interact with people when he is trapped at the bottom of this lake?"

thought Karen.

"You have found him and are talking with him. You can tell me whether he is now respectful or not. Does he still lie or is he honest? Does he cooperate with others or does he do what he thinks will best serve himself? Does he clean up the messes he makes or does he leave them for others? Does he feel gratitude or does he complain? Does he treat others with kindness or with cruelty? These are the tests he must pass before I will agree to release him."

Karen mentally sighed. "I would hope that Roggum would learn how to do these things. If you will set him free, he'll have a chance to prove himself. I have a feeling he won't disappoint you."

There was a long pause while the shaman considered Karen's suggestion. Then Roggum cleared his throat and spoke. "I know I can do it, this time! I'm sorry that I planned to trap you. Set me free, and let me help this special girl! She can tell you if I do anything wrong! Please, please! I've been punished enough! I've learned my lesson!"

The shaman looked from Roggum to Karen and after a long silence, he nodded. He then brought his hands together and slowly raised them in front of his body, and then swung them suddenly out wide to either side. As he did this, the orb burst and Roggum flew upwards amidst a flurry of bubbles to the surface of the lake.

Karen opened her eyes but couldn't see anything unusual on the lake, aside from many large bubbles rising together in the center.

"Thank you! Thank you! I am eternally in your debt!" cried Roggum, and Karen shut her eyes again to see him flying to embrace her. Another strong breeze swept past, and again the towel flapped. She couldn't help smiling as Roggum hugged her with his entire shaggy body, and she thought to him, "I'm so glad I could help you. Now it's up to you to help others."

Roggum lowered his head so low to the ground that it touched, and he said, "I am truly lucky to have been rescued by such a special girl. I will show you just how grateful and kind I can be! Please tell me how I can be of service!"

Karen grinned as Roggum bowed again and again, his head bobbing up and down like a furry yo-yo. "There might be one thing you could do to help."

"Anything! Give me a command!"

"I wish I could find out who put those explosives in a cave at the far side of the lake, and what they plan to do with them. Any information you can find about this would be very helpful."

"Your wish is my command!" Roggum squealed before flying off to the far side of the lake.

Be careful! Karen thought after him.

She opened her eyes as she felt a shadow pass over her face. It was Sondra, who was standing there shaking her head. "You look pale as a ghost. Would you like to return to your cabin and take a nap? Maybe you'll feel better after you get some sleep."

Karen nodded gratefully and walked back down the trail to the Turtle's cabin. Her body felt as heavy as the anchor on a boat, and she sank deeply into her sheets before falling sound asleep. She had the sense that someone was nearby, watching her, but she was too tired to figure out who it was and drifted off into a dream. After some time had passed, she had a terrible feeling that someone was trying to get into her body! She woke fully within her dream as she sensed that her very life depended on getting back into her body before she was taken over. The thought brought her to the ceiling above her bed, where she saw a figure, struggling to break her connection to her body and beat her inside. She recognized the cloaked figure immediately. It was Ohgeenay!

After so many encounters, Karen knew his cold, dark spirit by heart. He had the elements of strength, skill, and surprise on his side, and she was horrified to see that he was starting to wake her body up without her being fully in it. He was closer to her body than she was, and was blocking her from returning. Ohgeenay pushed on her body with great force, attempting to enter and awaken it with his spirit. He seemed to be making some headway, and Karen saw her body twitching in response.

"Help!" Karen cried out in desperation within her dream.

She heard a friendly spirit's voice reply, "I am here. Take a moment to remember that there is something you know better than Ohgeenay. You are much more familiar with getting into your body when you wake up than he is. You do this every day."

Karen was thrilled to be given this vital piece of information and realized it was true. She had woken up quickly thousands of times in her physical body and knew its brain and muscles much more intimately than Ohgeenay. She felt and saw a silvery cord that connected her dream body to her physical body that she could follow, so she knew she had the advantage over Ohgeenay.

With one precise lunge, she flew through the cord and dove into her body. Then she sat up in bed gasping for air, totally exhausted from the effort, but exhilarated to know that she'd done it. She'd outwitted Ohgeenay!

She heard him howling as he retreated into the darkness, and once again she sank back down into her covers. She felt that if Ohgeenay ever tried that trick again, she'd be ready. As she shut her eyes, she saw Ohgeenay flying away like a wounded animal, still howling with the agony of his defeat. She slept with confidence that she was well connected to her body, and that nobody else would take it over.

Karen was awakened by Roggum gently shaking her shoulder. "Wake up! Wake up! I have news for you!"

"What did you find out?" Karen asked drowsily.

"Good news and bad news. Which do you want to hear first?"

"How about the bad news first," Karen said, rubbing her eyes.

"The explosives are new and dangerous, and were placed in the cave with the intention to destroy the lake with a landslide of rocks from the mountain. I do not know who placed them there."

"WHY would someone plan to do such a thing?" asked Karen in horror.

"I do not know."

"And what is the good news?"

"Whoever put those new explosives in the cave did so recently, which means they are probably close by right now."

Karen felt hairs rising up all over her body. "If someone close by is preparing to destroy Lake Lovell swim camp, we have to stop them. Thank you for helping, Roggum."

"I helped? I really and truly helped?" Roggum beamed before starting to hop around the room in excitement.

Karen grinned at him as the cabin door swung open and her fellow Turtles returned to the cabin before lunchtime.

"Rise and shine!" Wanda said, as she pranced into the cabin. Ready for lunch? You missed all the excitement today!"

Karen smiled and replied, "I doubt it!"

Wanda raised one eyebrow curiously, and Karen laughed.

"Come on! I'll tell you all about it as we walk to lunch!"

Kirk Dempsey

Walking to the mess hall, Karen felt a tremendous sense of relief to be alive and well, and thankful to have a friend with whom to share her adventures. As Karen told her story, Wanda was uncharacteristically silent and didn't interrupt even once. "Now that Roggum is free, and Ohgeenay failed to take over my body," Karen concluded, "the only person we really need to concern ourselves with is the one who put the explosives in the cave."

Wanda shook her head in amazement. "That's the most awesome story I've ever heard. You really are something, Karen. But I don't see how you'll ever get someone to admit they put explosives in that cave and plan to blow up the mountain and destroy the lake."

Karen shrugged. "I have a feeling that someone will give themselves away." She and Wanda stopped at the end of the lunch line, where Julie and Gina were already standing. Karen poked Wanda. "There's Kirk! I'm going over to talk to him."

"Don't!" squealed Wanda, but Karen ignored her and strode purposefully over to where Kirk was standing in line.

"Hi, Kirk," Karen began, and then faltered when Kirk crossed his arms and turned away from her. She tried again in her sweetest tone of voice. "I just wanted to let you know that I wasn't the one who made that fake gum."

At this, Kirk spun around and glared at her for several seconds. Without saying a word, he stepped forward to the counter to take his tray. Karen returned to Wanda and Julie, looking dejected.

"That conversation went nowhere," Karen sighed.

"Why are you talking to *that* creep?" Julie demanded, "Isn't it obvious that he hates us?"

"Well, what you did to him was pretty mean," said Karen. "I can feel how angry he is, and I just wanted to let him know that he doesn't have to stay angry."

"Don't bother. His mind is already made up," Gina said, as the line moved forward. "The best thing to do is ignore him. This reminds me of what my mama says, *'Tanto va la gatta al lardo, che ci lascia lo zampino,'* which means, 'So much goes the cat to fat, that she leaves her little leg on it.'"

Karen furrowed her brows at Gina, wondering what she was getting at.

"I think in English you say, 'Don't push your luck,'" Gina explained.

"Maybe you're right," Karen sighed. "Talking to Kirk doesn't seem to do any good.

Karen sat down at the Turtle's table and picked at her lunch. Thinking about Kirk ruined her appetite. Sondra stopped by the table, leaned down and asked, "Are you feeling better, Karen? I notice you're not eating much."

"I'm feeling mostly better," Karen replied, "I think I can swim this afternoon."

"If you want to go back to the cabin, that will

146

be just fine," Sondra replied. "Listen to your body, and let me know how you're feeling. You can just cheer us on from the shore if you don't feel like racing."

Karen nodded and replied, "That sounds good."

"Great!" said Sondra, stroking Karen's hair and giving her a hug.

Karen finished as much of her lunch as she could stomach and brought her dishes to the counter. She was about to leave when she thought she saw Kirk smirk at her from the Flying Fish table and whisper something to one of his friends. She decided to follow Gina's advice, and ignore him.

Karen chose to watch the afternoon race from a restful place on the beach. She was sitting on a towel with one hand over her eyes when she was startled to see Digger Drummond walking over to her.

"Good afternoon, lassie!" Digger called out in a cheerful voice, removing his cap as he walked closer. "Catchin' some rays?"

Karen smiled up at him and said, "I'm feeling a bit sick today, so I'm just watching."

"It's good to know the limits of your body," Digger replied philosophically. He gazed out to see how the race was going. "Looks like your team could use a little help today."

Sure enough, the Turtles were not swimming their fastest. The Flying Fish were in the lead, and it seemed that this time they were winning fair and square.

"So how do you know Kirk?" Karen asked.

Digger put his cap back on his head and replied, "Kirk is me nephew. He's been comin' here every summer since he was seven years old. He used to tag along with me, but now I guess he's too grown-up for that."

Karen thought it was very lucky that Digger had shown up right when she was wondering how to reconcile things with Kirk.

"Kirk doesn't like me," Karen said, looking up at Digger for a reaction. "In fact, I have a feeling that he absolutely hates me."

Digger rocked backwards on his heels. "Oh, I doubt that, lassie. Kirk's had some bumps he has, and is angry about his lot in life. The lad may be a mite jealous that you have what he hankers for, but I dinna think he hates yeh."

Karen marveled that Kirk and Digger could be related. They seemed worlds apart. Digger's battered old clothes were as different from Kirk's blue and black coordinated outfits as could be, and while the grounds keeper's speech and mannerisms reminded Karen of someone from what her parents called, "the old country," Kirk was up on every trend.

"I don't know what Kirk would be jealous of," Karen said. "I am not a very good swimmer, and until I came here, my pet rat was my only real friend. Most of the time, I don't think my parents even like me."

"I canna say what makes one person jealous of another," Digger replied. He then lowered his voice and added, "The other possibility is that he's taken a fancy to yeh. Yeh are a bonny lass."

"If he liked me, would he be so mean to me?" Karen asked incredulously.

"I reckon so, if he doughtna ken a better way to get your attention."

Karen blushed and changed the subject.

"What's been the biggest change here at Lake Lovell over all the years?"

Digger looked off in the distance over the lake, and squinted his eyes at the bright reflections on the water. "Lots o' things be changing. Some things for the better, some not so much better. The world keeps getting more crowded with cities and cars, and then people miss the trees."

Karen nodded. *Could Digger be the one who put the explosives in the cave?* she wondered to herself. *Maybe he plans to blow the mountain up so people will leave this place alone.*

"What would happen if people stopped coming here?" she asked.

Digger turned to Karen with a piercing stare. "Now whatever could you mean by *that?*" he asked in a low voice. His gaze was so intense that Karen said, "Nothing!" before she had a chance to come up with a better response.

"Well, I gotta go back to my gardening!" Digger said, and with a slight bow and a tip of his cap, he sauntered away.

Karen flushed in frustration at having lost her chance to question Digger further. It was tricky to ask about the explosives without raising suspicions, and she'd managed to alarm Digger without mentioning either the cave or the explosives. *I'll have to find a way to raise the subject that doesn't make him so nervous,* Karen mused.

Karen looked back at the lake just as the race finished with the Flying Fish in first place, the Turtles in second place, and the Water Snakes in third. Karen was walking to join her fellow Turtles when Andy whistled and waved for her to come over. When she reached him, he whispered, "You know how I said you should be careful because Kirk is planning revenge?"

Karen nodded.

"I think whatever he's going to do, it's going to happen soon. I heard him tell his friend, Roger, that by this time tomorrow, it'll be all over."

"What will be all over? Did you hear anything more?" Karen asked in alarm.

"No, but I think he's going to do something terrible."

"Maybe you should tell somebody!" Karen exclaimed.

"There's nothing to tell yet. I don't want to be the tattletale. I'll keep listening, though, and let you know if I hear anything more," Andy said, as the others approached.

When Karen told Wanda what Andy had said, she looked really scared. "Yikes! Maybe we should tell Sondra."

"I thought of that," Karen said, "but Andy's right. Kirk really hasn't done anything, and I seriously doubt he's the one who hid explosives in the cave! Besides, what could Sondra possibly do? I think the best solution is just to pay attention and be careful."

Karen and Wanda changed quickly and, as the others engaged in wild talk about what Kirk might be up to, walked over to see Gill and Charlotte before dinner. Karen excitedly described how she'd helped to free Roggum and successfully fought off Ohgeenay. Then she mentioned what Roggum had told her about the explosives, and what Andy had told her about Kirk.

"You've had one busy day today, Karen!"

Charlotte said with a smile. "Sit down here, and I'll get you girls some cocoa."

For the first time all day, Karen felt like she could truly relax.

"Do you know what's going to happen?" Wanda asked Gill.

Gill just shook his head and said, "We all weave this web together. Anything is possible."

Karen had the feeling that Gill knew much more than he was saying, but also knew there was no point in getting him to elaborate.

Charlotte added, "Remember that we are never truly alone!" She winked at Karen as she said this, and Karen felt it was meant to be a clue.

"We can always call for help when we need it," Karen said.

Charlotte nodded and winked again.

After dinner, Karen fell sound asleep very quickly. When she awoke the next morning, she remembered she'd dreamed of her family. She missed them, and knew that in their own way, they missed her, too. In her dreams, she'd seen that her brothers had finished building their boxcar racer and took it up to the top of the hill on their street to try it out. She'd watched as they raced it down the street and swerved to miss a bicyclist, crashing it into a tree by the side of the road. Fortunately, the damage appeared to be minor, only affecting the right front side of the racer.

Karen rubbed her eyes, and looked at Gumdrop's cage to see whether he was awake, but he wasn't there! Her heart pounded, as she looked around the room. She knew he'd been there when she went to bed, and his cage door was shut. How could he have vanished?

"Gumdrop's gone!" Karen cried, as Wanda stretched in her bed nearby.

"What?"

"Gumdrop isn't in his cage, and I know he was there last night!"

Wanda jumped up to help Karen search the room. Julie and Gina and the others awakened, and soon all the Turtles were calling, "Gumdrop! Here, Gumdrop!"

"I think I know who took him!" Wanda said, "Kirk Dempsey!"

"Let's get dressed and go find him!" said Karen, jumping into her T-shirt and jeans as she spoke. Julie, Wanda, Karen, and Gina all headed out towards the lake.

"Hey, someone's out there in a rowboat!" Julie said, cupping her hands around her eyes to minimize the glare off the water. "It looks like one of the campers. It IS! It's a KID!"

Karen squinted at the silhouetted figure in the boat, wondering who would be crazy enough to take the rowboat out without permission at this hour. Whoever it was, they'd gone quite a distance already, and stopped rowing. The oar was set inside the boat, and something small was scooped up and held high over the water.

Karen had a sinking feeling that this was the horrible thing she'd dreamt about. She was flooded by a sense of déjà vu, sure that this had happened before in a dream. She squinted harder as Julie breathlessly exclaimed, "Wow! Kirk kidnapped Gumdrop and is going to feed him to the monster in the lake!"

"I'm getting Sondra!" cried Wanda, running

back to the cabins before anyone could reply.

"*Misericordia*," was all that Gina had to say, as she and Karen gazed out over the water and saw that Julie's assessment was most likely true. Karen felt like sobbing and she wanted to scream Gumdrop's name, but knew that neither of these things was going to help. What had Charlotte said just a few minutes earlier that she could do when things went very badly? This surely was just such a moment.

Karen shut her eyes and tried to calm herself. She noticed for the first time that she couldn't seem to stop shaking, and that her breathing was coming in rapid, ragged gasps. She reminded herself that she'd felt panicky before, and everything had turned out all right. What did she do to make it turn out all right? Karen couldn't remember. Her mind was a blank, and she felt her body spasm with shakes. She focused on taking big, slow deep breaths. She felt how much she loved Gumdrop and how much he loved her. She felt how special they were to each other. If only someone could come to help Gumdrop.

That was it! Charlotte had said that all she ever had to do was ask, and help was with her. If ever there were a time she needed help, this was it. In her mind, Karen cried out, "HELP! Save Gumdrop! Bring him safely back to me!" Her mind and heart cried out in unison as she helplessly watched Kirk dangling Gumdrop over the side of the rowboat, suspended just inches above the water. She felt all her love for her beloved pet. Remembering how sweetly he'd been sleeping in his Kleenex box just an hour ago melted her heart. Suddenly there was a burst of light like the flash on a camera going off, and Karen sensed a presence of love near her.

She heard voices behind her as Mr. Drummond returned with Wanda. "They're out in the boat!" Wanda gasped, pointing at the distant figures.

"Kirk? Is that really Kirk out there?" asked Digger, in disbelief. "What is he doing out on the water at this hour?"

"He's got Karen's pet rat, and he's gonna drown him!" shouted Julie.

"Ah don' believe it!" exclaimed Digger, squinting for a better view. "HEY! KIRK! WHAT IN BLAZES ARE YOU DOIN' OUT THERE?" he shouted. At the boom of his voice echoing across the lake, Kirk looked up for the first time to notice he had an audience on shore.

Karen and the others could see the boy in the boat seem to change his mind. He brought the small rodent back inside the boat and set him down. Then he picked up the oars and began rowing back to shore. Karen could hardly believe her eyes. Gumdrop was safe!

Charisse Chapman

"You lassies go ahead and take the little guy home, while I drag this one to see the camp director for his comeuppance," Mr. Drummond said, putting one arm around Kirk's slouched shoulders to wheel him off in the direction of ChaCha's cabin. In spite of her anger, Karen almost felt sorry for Kirk.

Karen was surrounded by friends as the girls pressed in close to see Gumdrop. They all spoke at once.

"I think he's dizzy!"

"No, he's not. He just woke up too early."

"He looks seasick to me!"

When Karen gazed into her little rat's gentle eyes, she sensed that he was none the worse for his harrowing experience. She felt guilty for not waking up when Kirk had come into the Turtles cabin and kidnapped him, and wondered how he could have done that without anyone noticing.

Julie echoed this unspoken question. "How come no one noticed Kirk sneaking around in our cabin last night?"

The other Turtles all shook their heads, and Karen replied, "I think he must have been very quiet. He knew exactly what he was after, and Gumdrop's cage is right in front of the window. Gumdrop trusts people, and wouldn't put up much of a struggle or even squeak out in alarm if someone picked him up."

Karen put her pet up on her shoulder, and he snuggled down in her long blonde hair. Wanda, Julie and Gina strolled along beside her, reaching over occasionally to pet Gumdrop between Karen's locks of hair.

"Kirk is in BIG trouble now!" said Gina.

Julie laughed. "Yeah, I bet he'll have to do chores around the camp in all his spare time for the rest of the week. That's what happened last year when he flushed Kimberly Brown's watch down the toilet!"

As she climbed the wooden stairs to the Turtles cabin, Karen shuddered to realize how close Gumdrop had come to being dropped into the depths of Lake Lovell. He looked relieved to be return to his cage and familiar nesting box, scampering through the open door and heading directly to his water bottle for a long drink. Karen stroked his soft fur before latching the cage shut, then left with the rest for breakfast.

"I never heard the story about Kimberly's watch. What happened?" asked Wanda.

"There's not much to tell, Julie said. "Kimberly set her watch down on a towel by the beach, and when she wasn't looking, Kirk took it. When Kimberly came back after swimming, she noticed the watch was gone, and later that day Kirk bragged that he'd flushed it down the toilet. Since the watch was gone, and Kirk admitted that he was the one who took it, he got in BIG trouble and ended up scrubbing toilets for days!"

"Wow," said Wanda, "that's much worse than anything I've ever done. The worst thing I ever did was to shake up a can of soda pop so it sprayed all over my sister's T-shirt – when she was wearing it! I got in big trouble for that, but I would never dream of flushing something down the toilet. I wonder what made Kirk think he'd get away with that."

Julie explained, "ChaCha said that Kirk likes the attention and until he learns to make friends, he'll probably keep doing mean things just so people don't ignore him."

"But Kirk has many friends," protested Gina. "All the Flying Fish, they do just what he says."

"But those aren't real friends," said Karen. "Those guys are just intimidated because Kirk is a bully.

"Well, he'll never make real friends if he keeps acting like that!" exclaimed Wanda indignantly.

Julie shrugged. "True enough. ChaCha said it's a vicious cycle, whatever that means."

Sondra had been standing by the mess hall door waiting for Karen. She greeted her by saying, "I heard what happened to Gumdrop, Karen. I'm so glad your rat is safe and sound! Come with me; we need to go see ChaCha."

Karen walked with Sondra to the camp director's office. Even though she knew she wasn't the one who was in trouble, she still felt very nervous. ChaCha's cabin smelled mustier and older than the Turtle's cabin or Gill and Charlottes. It was if all the smells that had ever wafted in had decided to remain rather than blow out again. ChaCha was seated in a large armchair facing Kirk Dempsey who was on the sofa. ChaCha indicated the sofa to Karen with the sweep of her arm, and Karen sat down next to Kirk. Sondra sat in another armchair alongside.

"Thanks for coming," ChaCha said to Karen and Sondra. Karen noticed that Steve was also present, standing on the other side of the sofa by Kirk. He stood straight and tall, looking more like a department store mannequin than a person until his nose itched, and he rubbed it. Mr. Drummond also stood behind the sofa, leaning against the wall and fidgeting with his cap.

"I was deeply distressed to hear that Karen's pet rat had been taken from her cabin this morning," ChaCha began. "And I was even more upset when I heard that Kirk had taken him out on the lake and tormented both him and you, Karen. What Kirk did was inexcusable, and he has agreed that he will work on camp chores for a full day after swim camp ends, and that he will apologize to Karen for taking her pet."

All eyes turned to Kirk, who looked down at the floor. "I am sorry for taking your rat," he said so softly that Karen could barely hear him.

Her face flushed red as she replied, "Thanks for giving him back to me."

ChaCha gave Karen a look that asked if she wished to say anything more.

Karen cleared her throat and said, "There is something else I need to talk to you about."

"Yes?" asked ChaCha.

Karen paused for a moment to gather her courage. This was the perfect moment to mention the explosives, since four adults were gathered together as witnesses. "Someone I trust told me there are new boxes of explosives stored in a cave on the far side of Lake Lovell." Karen's face flushed hot, as her words came out in a rush.

"Who told you this?" ChaCha asked in alarm.

"A friend. I think you might want to check it out."

Steve surprised Karen by leaping forward and saying, "Allow me. I'll take the boat out across the lake before the afternoon races begin."

"I'll go with you," Digger volunteered, with a look of somber reserve on his face.

"Be careful not to touch anything," ChaCha warned," because explosives can be highly unstable. Let me know what the situation is, and then I will notify the authorities."

Both men nodded, and rushed from the room.

"Do they know where the cave is?" Karen asked.

"I'm sure they can find a cave, if one is there. Either way, I'll call the police as soon as they come back."

Karen thought to herself, *you mean IF they come back.*

After several painful moments of silence, ChaCha gazed first at Karen and then Kirk, and said, "Fortunately, no irreparable harm seems to have come from this morning's inconsiderate prank. I hope that this last day of swim camp will be a good one for all of us and that we can shake hands and agree to treat each other with respect." She gave Kirk an especially pointed look and said, "I'll be keeping an eye on you, Buster!"

Karen walked back to the mess hall with Sondra as Kirk followed a few paces behind.

"This is the last day of our races," Sondra reminded Karen, "and the day that the Lovell Cup will go to one of the teams. We have a chance of winning, as long as you join us and do your best!"

Karen looked up at Sondra, feeling glad that she could see the day in a fresh new way that wasn't overshadowed by the events of the morning. "I'll swim my fastest!" she promised.

ChaCha signaled an announcement at breakfast that morning by leaping up on top of a dining room bench and blowing her golden whistle. "This is the last day of swim camp, so I want to remind you that today's relay race will determine who takes the Lovell Cup! Last year, the cup went to the Flying Fish," ChaCha gestured towards their table as a roar went up from the boys who pounded the table with their fists and stomped their feet. When the racket subsided, the director continued, "This year's races have been very close, so I expect you all to swim your very best today!"

Karen closed her eyes, and sensed Roggum's warm furry body wrapped snugly around her own. She smiled as she heard him say, "I am so glad I could help you this morning! I got Mr. Drummond right away, and he saw what that bad boy was doing!"

Karen replied in thought. "Thank you, Roggum! I thought that might have been you!" She could see Roggum's eyes shut in ecstasy as he curled his toes and clapped his shaggy arms together. He opened them and did a couple of cartwheels before saying, "So you can tell the big shaman that I have been kind and helpful just when you needed me most!"

"Yes, I will tell him!" thought Karen, as she opened her eyes.

She saw all the other Turtles were clearing their dishes off the table and heading for the door, so she got up to follow. She noticed Kirk a few steps in front of her. He turned, as if he'd sensed someone watching him, and gave Karen a sad, wary look. She extended her right hand and said, "I just want to say that I hope we can be friends."

Kirk stood still, watching her for what felt like an eternity. One corner of his mouth turned up in a crooked smile, as he took her hand in his and shook it firmly. "I'd like that."

Karen felt her cheeks were flushing red again, so she gave him a quick smile and turned to follow the other Turtles to the lake. "See you out there!" she called back to the rather perplexed boy, who stood as still as a statue by the dish counter, watching her walk out the door.

The Cave

When Karen reached the lake, she was surprised to see the Flying Fish milling about. "Have you seen Steve?" Andy asked as she approached.

"The last time I saw him was in ChaCha's office before breakfast," Karen began. "He and Digger Drummond went out on the boat to investigate something."

"I saw Steve take the boat across the lake," said Sondra, "but he was the only one aboard."

Karen had a terrible feeling in the pit of her stomach. "They were supposed to go together," she said, gazing at the boat pulled ashore on the far side of the lake.

"EEEEK!" shrieked a girl from the River Otters team, who was standing by the trees along the shore.

Karen, Sondra, and Andy rushed along with dozens of others to see what frightened her.

"Unnghnh…" groaned the low voice of someone in incredible pain. "Where in blazes am I?!" A bedraggled Digger Drummond sat up slowly holding one hand to his head.

"You're bleeding!" exclaimed Sondra. "Stay right there, and I'll get a wet towel for your head."

"One minute I was walking around the boat to give her a push on out, and the next I find meself here in the bushes."

"What happened to Steve?" asked Karen, gripped by a sudden overwhelming sense of raw terror.

"I have no idea," groaned Digger. "I kinna believe he hit me in the head with an oar."

Karen took off running for ChaCha's cabin, and rushed inside to breathlessly announce, "Digger's hurt. I think Steve hit him with an oar, and might be getting ready to blow up the mountain right now!"

ChaCha stared at Karen for what seemed like an eternity, before saying, "Slow down and tell me how you know what you know about the explosives."

Karen recounted everything, beginning with her first dream of the petroglyphs and including her secret swim to the far side of the lake, to confirm that what she'd dreamt was true. "I can feel that Steve is scared, and that he might do something really foolish," Karen finished, hoping against hope that ChaCha would believe what must seem like an incredible story.

"I'll call the police now," ChaCha said, picking up the phone to place the call. "Stay here so you can tell them where to find the cave when they arrive."

Karen collapsed into a chair, and immediately felt Roggum's presence nearby. "You found him! You found the one who hid the explosives!" Roggum exclaimed in delight.

"Yes," Karen replied in her thoughts. "But I may have found him too late. He's across the lake right now, feeling terrified. At first I thought his terror was my own, it's not. He's so scared right now that he might blow the mountain up."

"Not if Roggum stops him!" Roggum countered. "Tell me what to do!"

"If you could get him to walk out of the cave and away from the explosives, he'd be less likely to blow up the mountain," began Karen, "and then help will be here soon."

"Consider it done!" cried Roggum, flying off at top speed.

ChaCha hung up the phone and said, "They're on their way. I would hardly have believed you, except that legend has it that there is a cave on the far side of the lake, and Digger has been injured. Do you get a feeling now from Steve – of what he is doing?"

"I can feel how frightened he is – at first I thought that was me being frightened, but it's him. I also feel that he may soon come back out toward the entrance to the cave, away from the explosives."

Just as Karen spoke, she saw in her mind's eye an image of Roggum tripping Steve inside the cave. Steve's flashlight flew out of his hands as he fell, and broke when it hit the rocky floor of the cave. "I can see Steve in the dark inside of the cave, turning around to go back down the steps."

Karen was surprised to see that ChaCha continued listening with rapt attention. "Do you know why Steve hid the explosives in the cave?" ChaCha asked.

Karen began to say "No," but as soon as the question was asked, she sensed she did know the answer. She saw an image of Steve finding the boxes of explosives in a nearby warehouse, and bringing them in his pick-up truck one dark night to hide them in the cave. The next image she saw of Steve was in bright daylight, and he was on television! He was combing his hair back and talking to a news reporter about how he'd been lucky to be on the scene to rescue swim campers when a horrible earthquake shook the mountain into the lake and the swim camp. "He wanted to be a hero on TV," Karen said, shaking her head in wonder. "He found the explosives and thought it would be easy to use them to cause a disaster, so he hid them in the cave until he got up enough nerve to blow up the mountain."

The door to ChaCha's office opened and two police officers walked inside, accompanied by a German shepherd.

"I'm so glad to see you, officers!" ChaCha exclaimed. "You arrived so quietly I didn't hear you at all."

"We're here to look for explosives," the taller of the two policemen replied. "We arrived with sirens and lights off."

"Yes, of course. Follow us, and Karen will describe how you can find the cave."

Karen described the cave entrance to the policemen, and from the safety of the beach, watched the officers and their dog cross the lake in a rowboat. When they reached the shore, she saw them walk directly to the cave and arrest Steve, who was crouched just inside the mouth of the cave. The taller of the two policemen took the dog inside the cave, and when he re-emerged, brought his prisoner back to shore with his wrists handcuffed behind his back. The other policeman remained at the cave.

Steve was silent and glum as he was led

away. "I bet this isn't the way he hoped to look when he first appeared on TV," Karen commented to Wanda.

"I don't think they even let him comb his hair," Wanda giggled.

Once Digger recovered from his mild concussion, he was able to remember how Steve had hit him with an oar. The officers took many notes before driving away with Steve in the back of the patrol car. "I'll be back to retrieve the explosives. Please keep everyone away from the cave," he said before driving away.

The morning practice seemed surreal after the unusual events of the morning, but Karen felt proud of how well she was swimming. She'd learned how to do the butterfly, the backstroke, and the Australian crawl, although she was best at a free style hybrid. All the Turtles were swimming faster than they'd started, and Karen noticed how proud Miranda seemed of her fellow teammates now. Miranda was unquestionably the fastest Turtle, and her example set the pace for the rest.

Lunchtime came all too soon, and Karen realized how much she would miss her new friends. She went to visit Gill and Charlotte one last time as they prepared lunch in the kitchen. "I am going to miss you so much," she sniffled as tears ran down her cheeks. Karen hadn't meant to cry, but she couldn't help feeling the loss of her newfound family.

Charlotte wrapped her arms around Karen and hugged her as the tears continued to flow.

Gill said, "You can't miss us when you don't go away."

Karen lifted her head out of Charlotte's

loving embrace and blinked back her tears to see Gill more clearly. "What do you mean?" she asked.

"You are at home here with us, and your heart is here. You can't ever go away entirely when you leave your heart behind."

"We will always be with you, in your heart, just as you will always be with us," Charlotte added. Tears began to well up again and Karen's voice choked as she said, "But I will miss you SO much."

Charlotte held Karen in a long embrace allowing seconds and then minutes to flow on by around them as Gill continued to prepare lunch.

When it was time to eat, Karen gave Gill a hug and then walked over to the mess hall line without looking back. She didn't want to start crying again.

The Lovell Cup

So many parents had arrived to watch the final race that there wasn't enough room for them all on the small set of bleachers. Fortunately, most came prepared and seated themselves on folding chairs and beach towels they'd brought along. When Karen left the mess hall after lunch, she spotted her mother's red straw hat and red and white striped dress immediately and waved. Kimball saw her and waved back. There wasn't time for more than a quick hug before Karen had to run and suit up.

Wanda's parents had both come to watch the final race, and Wanda pointed them out to Karen. She smiled. It seemed like all over the camp people were waving.

"I've got butterflies in my stomach!" Karen said to Wanda as she looked at the other teams, wondering if others felt as nervous as she did.

"Me, too" said Wanda.

ChaCha stood regally before the assembled crowd in her spectacular golden swimsuit. She blew her golden whistle and addressed the crowd. "I'd like to thank all the parents for coming out to watch our race today, and our swim instructors for doing such an excellent job of training our campers. Many campers came here just four weeks ago not knowing how to swim, and today will be competing against some of the very best! I know that you will be proud of them. I certainly am."

ChaCha turned to the lake and raised one arm high above her head for dramatic effect. "And now, we are ready for the final race of the week. The winner of today's race will be awarded the highest honor Lake Lovell's swim camp has to offer, the Lovell Cup! This is the moment we've been preparing for all month. This is it, campers. Give it all you've got. Now! ON YOUR MARKS. GET SET. GO!" She dropped her hand, and the race began.

Karen awaited her turn to swim with eager anticipation. It seemed to take forever for the first few swimmers to pass the purple band, and finally Karen was at the front of the line watching Julie swim toward her holding the bracelet. She dug her toes into the warm sand, thinking that today she would use the Australian crawl and telling herself over and over that she could swim faster than she ever had before. She'd spent all her spare time the day before imagining herself doing the crawl, and now that the moment was here, the butterflies were gone and she was feeling good about it.

Julie was now within a few feet and closing in fast. Karen leaned forward to grasp the band, and she was off! She snapped the bracelet around her wrist, took a huge breath of air and lunged forward. With every stroke of her arms, she felt like she was pulling herself just a bit faster than ever before, and kicked with all the strength she could muster. Finally, she sensed rather than saw that Wanda was just a few feet away, her hand extended to take the band. Karen handed it over.

She clung to the raft and watched Wanda butterfly back to shore. She couldn't help but grin at the thought of how just a few weeks ago, Wanda had been worried about drowning when she did the dog paddle. Now she could back stroke and butterfly with the best of them. Karen knew that her own swimming was much better, too, and figured she'd made it to the raft almost as fast as Miranda did.

Two short blasts of ChaCha's whistle announced the end of the race. The Turtles had finished first, which meant that they'd won the cup! Karen and the other Turtles yelled for joy, and all the swimmers out on the raft came back in to shore to hear ChaCha's official announcement.

Karen was almost knocked off-balance by Wanda and Julie and Gina as they all ran up to hug her at the same time. Wanda couldn't contain her excitement and broke free to dance a high-stepping jig of joy.

ChaCha's whistle blew again, and a silence fell across the crowd so they could hear her final announcement. "Today's race was won by the Turtles, which means they are also the winners of the Lake Lovell Swim Cup! Turtles, please step forward to receive your ribbons!"

The crowd parted to allow Karen and her teammates to step forward to the pier where ChaCha was standing. She presented each swimmer with a brass "First Place" medallion hung on a blue ribbon necklace. When Karen stepped forward to receive her award, ChaCha said, "Congratulations, Turtles! Well done!" Karen flushed with pride, and stepped back down. Out of the corner of her eye she could see her mother waving to her, and she waved back. She examined the picture on her brass medallion, and was pleased to see that it was an image of Lovell Lake with the mountains behind it, surrounded by trees.

When all Turtles had received their ribbons, ChaCha continued, "Second place and the red ribbons go to the Flying Fish. Come on up to receive your medallions."

Andy grinned from ear to ear and waved at Karen as he stepped forward to receive his medallion. Then Karen caught Kirk's eye. She saw him flush slightly and turn towards ChaCha to receive his prize. When he stepped back, he looked at Karen once again and blushed even more. He turned to walk away, but glanced back at Karen one last time, as if he were mentally photographing her so he could remember the moment forever.

When ChaCha was done awarding the Water Snakes and River Otters their medals, every swim camper was wearing a colorful ribbon necklace with a shining medallion.

"Last but not least, I'd like to inform you that the Lovell Cup remains here at Lake Lovell. This year it will be placed in the Turtles cabin. I hope that we'll be seeing you back here again next year. Have a wonderful time for the rest of the summer!"

With that, ChaCha bounded down off the pier, and the swimmers joined their families. Karen's mother embraced her in a stifling hug and said, "I'm so proud of you, my little mermaid!"

Karen blushed in embarrassment about being called a mermaid, but was grateful to realize that none of the other campers would know what Mrs. Kimball was referring to. "I can't believe it! You won first place!"

Karen was unaccustomed to her mother expressing pride in her accomplishments, and was unsure how to respond. She blushed a little, then said, "You were right, Mom. I learned how to swim and made some friends, just like you said!" She didn't feel she could tell her mother the parts about Roggum, Makai-mo, Ohgeenay, Kirk, and the Shortgrasses, but she felt Roggum give her a furry all-over hug the moment she thought of him. "I'll be with you wherever you go, and I won't let you down!" he squawked.

Karen laughed in spite of herself. How odd to be standing next to her mother and seeing Roggum doing cartwheels all around her. "If she only knew," thought Karen.

Mrs. Kimball finally released her daughter from the smothering hug just as Wanda bounced up. "I just want to tell you that you're the best swim partner ever!" she squealed.

"Who is your little friend?" Mrs. Kimball asked Karen, "She's so cute!"

Karen blushed with embarrassment, and said, "Mother, this is Wanda! Wanda, this is Mrs. Kimball – my mom!"

Wanda extended her hand as Mrs. Kimball grasped it and pulled her in to one of the smothering hugs. "Any friend of Karen's is a friend of mine!" she exclaimed.

From deep within Mrs. Kimball's arms came the muffled reply, "So pleased to meet you!"

Just then Andy and Ben walked over. "We just want to say how great it was to meet you, and we hope we'll get to see you again soon,"

Andy said to Karen.

Karen nodded, ignoring Mrs. Kimball's raised eyebrow and quizzical look. She knew her mother was wondering if the twins were both her boyfriends. Karen smiled at the twins and called back, "Have a great summer!" as they waved and walked away.

Mrs. Kimball opened her mouth to speak, but Karen didn't give her a chance. "Just friends," she said blushing slightly.

After several rounds of tearful hugs and promises to write, one by one the campers collected their belongings and climbed into cars with their families.

Mrs. Kimball babbled happily about her days as a Musical Mermaid as she started up the car and began driving slowly down the gravel road. "Did I ever tell you about the time we were awarded the key to the city?" she gushed. "We were the toast of the town! We had our pictures taken for the newspaper, and performed our synchronized swim routine every weekend for the entire summer."

Karen just smiled and listened. Then she asked, "How are Decker and Tad? I bet they tried their boxcar racer and crashed it already!"

"How did you know THAT?!" exclaimed Mrs. Kimball. "As a matter of fact, they just finished it the other day. They took it up to the top of the hill, and when they swerved to miss a little boy on a bike, they hit a tree!"

"Minor damage on the right front side of their box car, right?" Karen was enjoying this.

"That's right! But Decker says he'll have it good as new by this time next week." Mrs. Kimball shook her head. "Frankly, I wish it had been destroyed. Dangerous that thing is. Dangerous. Now I suppose they'll go find a taller hill to try it out on!"

Karen looked down at Gumdrop, and thought, *Mom has no idea how alive and connected everything is.*

Gumdrop gripped the bars on his cage as the car bumped along the river access road. Karen was certain she heard him reply, "No idea. Absolutely no idea at all!"

About the Author

Cynthia Sue Larson is the author of several books about the ways consciousness changes the physical world. She publishes the RealityShifters ezine at her web site: *www.RealityShifters.com*